P9-BBO-955

ANOTHER KIND

CAIT MAY & TREVOR BREAM

HARPER alley
An Imprint of HarperCollinsPublishers

CHAPTER ONE

WE KNOW WHAT YOU ARE

NO ENTRY
PRIVATE PROPERTY
NO TRESPASSING
tmp
tmp
tmp
NO ENTRY
DUCK
CHING
CHING
PRIVATE PROPERTY
NO
TRESPASSIN

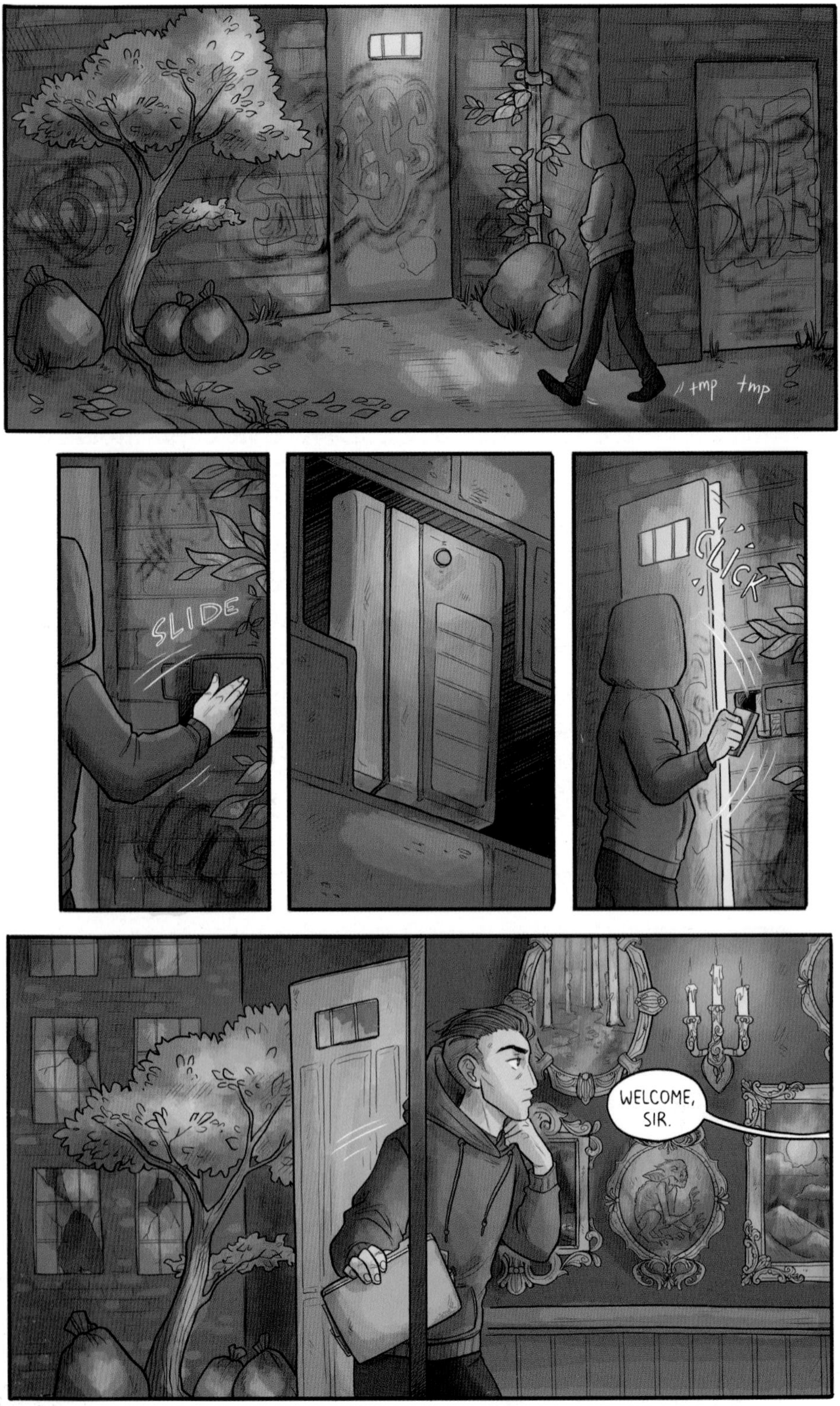
tmp tmp
SLIDE
CLICK
WELCOME, SIR.

THE MASTER IS EXPECTING YOU.
WILL YOU TAKE TEA OR COFFEE?
NEITHER, THANK YOU. I'M FINE.
VERY WELL, SIR. ONE MOMENT, I'LL LET HIM KNOW YOU'VE ARRIVED.
nod
fwip
HERE YOU ARE, SIR.

...WELL?

I HAVE AS MUCH AS I FELT SAFE LEAVING WITH.
I DON'T WANT THE OTHER AGENTS TO GET SUSPICIOUS.
THAT WOULD BE RATHER COUNTER-PRODUCTIVE.
...YES.
AS YOU SEE, THESE ARE THE **IRREGULARITIES** WE SPOKE ABOUT.
SIX OF THEM?
YES, SIR. THE YOUNGEST IS SIX YEARS OLD, AND THE ELDEST IS SIXTEEN.
I HAVE COPIES OF THEIR DOSSIERS AND SOME PHOTOS.
TELL ME MORE.

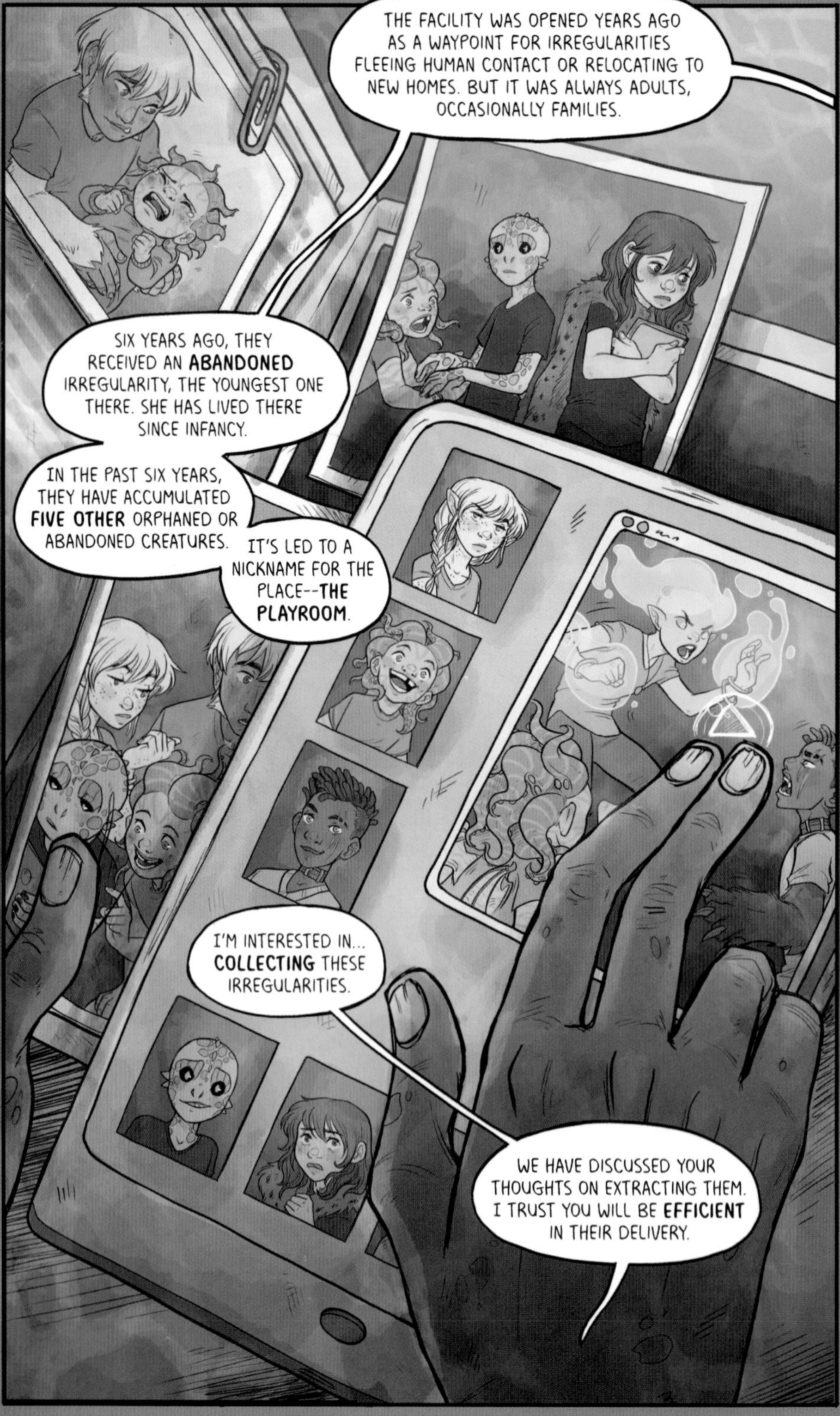
THE FACILITY WAS OPENED YEARS AGO AS A WAYPOINT FOR IRREGULARITIES FLEEING HUMAN CONTACT OR RELOCATING TO NEW HOMES. BUT IT WAS ALWAYS ADULTS, OCCASIONALLY FAMILIES.
SIX YEARS AGO, THEY RECEIVED AN **ABANDONED** IRREGULARITY, THE YOUNGEST ONE THERE. SHE HAS LIVED THERE SINCE INFANCY.
IN THE PAST SIX YEARS, THEY HAVE ACCUMULATED **FIVE OTHER** ORPHANED OR ABANDONED CREATURES.
IT'S LED TO A NICKNAME FOR THE PLACE--**THE PLAYROOM**.
I'M INTERESTED IN... **COLLECTING** THESE IRREGULARITIES.
WE HAVE DISCUSSED YOUR THOUGHTS ON EXTRACTING THEM. I TRUST YOU WILL BE **EFFICIENT** IN THEIR DELIVERY.

SIR...
SIR, ABOUT MY PAYMENT?
YOU WILL RECEIVE YOUR DUE, MY GOOD MAN. I DON'T LEAVE MY ASSETS **UNSATISFIED**.
ahem
I WILL BE KEEPING THESE FILES. AND YOU WILL BRING ME MORE INFORMATION ABOUT THEIR MOVEMENTS.
ACQUIRING THESE SIX COULD BE A CHALLENGE. WITH YOUR ASSISTANCE, I TRUST IT WILL NOT BE SO.
SIR... UH... YES. ONCE **PAYMENT** IS RECEIVED.
AND PERHAPS I SHOULD HOLD ON TO THE INFORMATION...
IN THE WRONG HANDS MY IDENTITY COULD BE COMPROMIS--

SLAM
SHATTER
DO NOT MISUNDERSTAND ME, SIR!
YOU ARE EXPENDABLE. IF YOU ARE COMPROMISED I WILL FIND MYSELF ANOTHER DECEITFUL WORM TO DO YOUR JOB.
QUESTION ME AGAIN AND YOU WILL BE WORRYING ABOUT MUCH MORE THAN PAYMENT.
DO I MAKE MYSELF ABUNDANTLY CLEAR?
drip
drip
shffff

REPORT BACK THE MOMENT YOU HAVE WHAT I NEED.
Y-YES, SIR.
YES, SIR.
wave
drip drip
HMM.
CHILD IRREGULARITIES.
THIS SHOULD PROVE INTERESTING.

GASP!
GOOD MORNING, SLEEPYHEAD!
GGRRMPH...
OW OW OW OW OW
flop

WAKE UUUPPP, WAKE UP WAKE UP WAKE UP!
BAPPITA BAPPITA BAPPITA
GGRRAAAA-
DUDE, YOU'VE GOT MORNING BREATH.
baff
ALL RIGHT, PIPSQUEAK. I'M UP.
GET OFF.
GOOD! I THOUGHT YOU WERE GONNA SLEEP **FOREVER**.
BREAKFAST TIIIIME!
J
N
YAAAAWN
M
EVERYBODY **WAKE UP**!!!!

NEWT! JAALI! BREAKFAST TIME! THINK OF THE COCOA PUFFS!
bang
bang
OOH! COCOA PUFFS!
COME ON!
EVERY... SINGLE... DAY...
I HAVEN'T HAD TO SET AN ALARM CLOCK IN SIX YEARS.
YAAAAAWN
HECK YEAH, COCOA PUFFS!

PLEASE TELL ME THERE'S SOMETHING NEW ON THE SCHEDULE TODAY?
NOPE, SAME AS USUAL. LESSONS IN THE MORNING, PRACTICE THIS AFTER-NOON.
THEN YOU HAVE SOME STUDY TIME TONIGHT, AND DINNER.
SUCH VARIETY! I CAN HARDLY CONTAIN MYSELF!
WELL, I LIKE PRACTICE.
Y'KNOW, IF I COULD TURN INTO A BEAR I WOULD PROBABLY LIKE PRACTICE TOO.
PFF. YOU CAN FLY! WHAT'S MORE FUN THAN THAT?
IT'S NOT AS EASY AS IT LOOKS, ALL RIGHT?
WELL, I'M GLAD WE HAVE SOME FREE TIME TO STUDY! WE HAVE TO GET READY FOR MIDTERMS!
...WHAT?

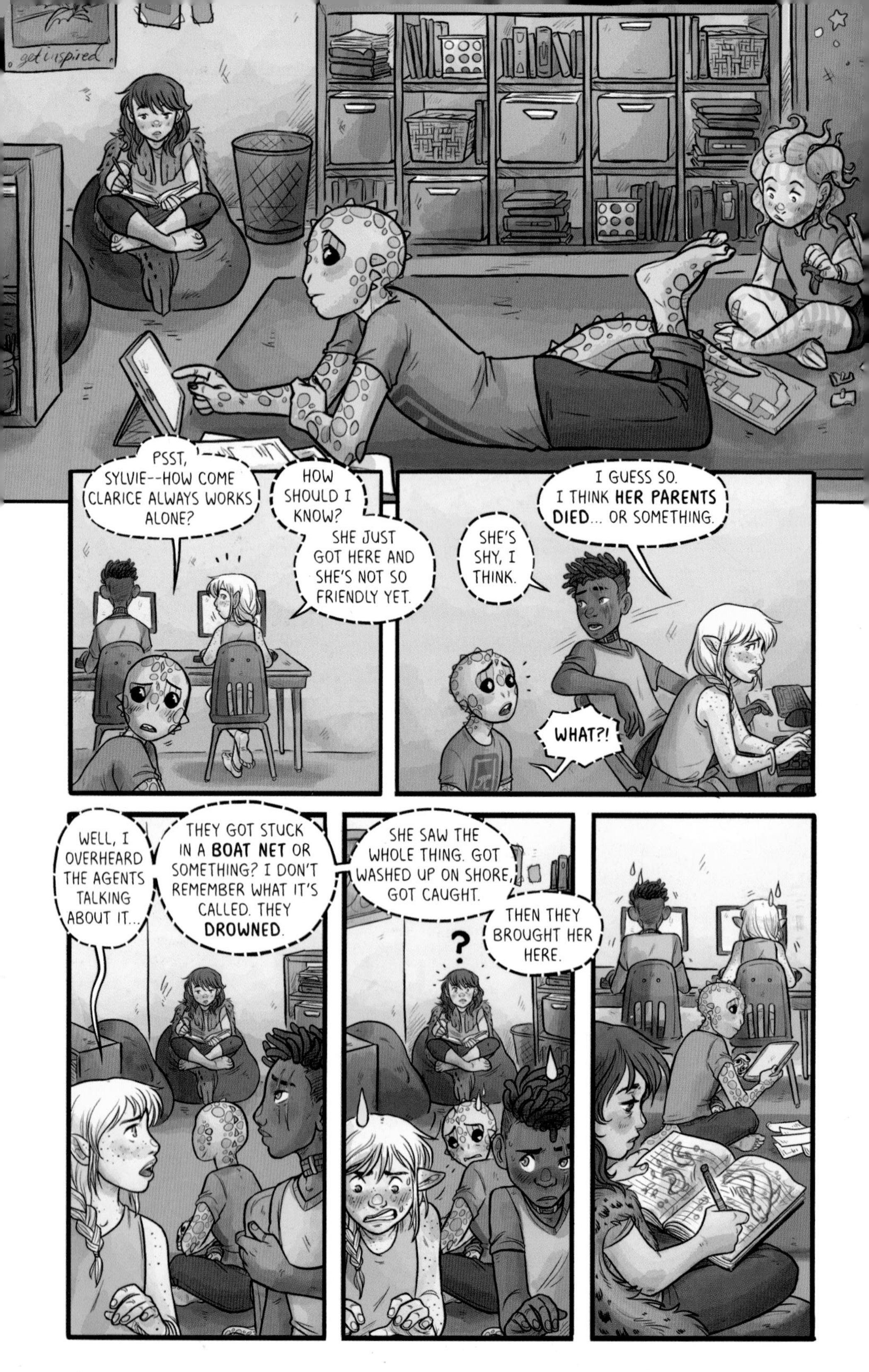
get inspired
PSST, SYLVIE--HOW COME CLARICE ALWAYS WORKS ALONE?
HOW SHOULD I KNOW?
SHE JUST GOT HERE AND SHE'S NOT SO FRIENDLY YET.
SHE'S SHY, I THINK.
I GUESS SO. I THINK **HER PARENTS DIED**... OR SOMETHING.
WHAT?!
WELL, I OVERHEARD THE AGENTS TALKING ABOUT IT...
THEY GOT STUCK IN A **BOAT NET** OR SOMETHING? I DON'T REMEMBER WHAT IT'S CALLED. THEY **DROWNED**.
SHE SAW THE WHOLE THING. GOT WASHED UP ON SHORE, GOT CAUGHT.
THEN THEY BROUGHT HER HERE.
?

UGH!
OMAR--WHERE DOES WISCONSIN GO?
OMAR.
OMAR?!
OMAR OMAR OMAR OMAR OMAR OMAR
WHAT?
WHERE DOES WISCONSIN GO??
I DON'T KNOW, NORTH SOMEWHERE?
YOU'RE NOT HELPING.

INH ALE
clap clap clap clap
SPLASH!
OOOH! THAT ONE WAS PRETTY!
ptoo!
ACK! HEY, QUIT IT!
HA HA HA HA HA HA
sspppt!

HEY, NEWT!
HEY, AGENT RAMIREZ!
TIME FOR YOU TO PRACTICE TOO. HOP UP-- LET'S SEE YOU **SHIFT**.
AWH... DO I HAVE TO?
YEP. YOUR **FATHER** WANTS YOU TO PRACTICE EVERY DAY.
...
OKAYYY...
IT'S OKAY, NEWT! I BET YOU'LL GET IT THIS TIME!
stuff
foof
shff
LOOK!! I **DID IT**!!
NOT... QUITE, NEWT.
HUH? WHAT DO YOU MEAN?
AWH MAN.

...10...11...12...
GOOD ENOUGH?
WE DONE HERE?
huff huff
YEP, GO COOL OFF.
YES!!
WHUMP!
WHOOOOAAA!
WOOOOow!
KA-SPLOOSH!
HA HA HA HA HA
HA HA HA HA HA HA
JAALI, NO RUNNING BY THE POOL. YOU KNOW BETTER.

EWW! WET BEAR SMELL!
BOO!
MADE YA JUMP.
NO YOU DIDN'T.
HOW'S IT HANGIN'?
OH, Y'KNOW. JUST PULLING MYSELF UP BY SHEER WILL HERE.
NOT LIKE I NEED TO **CONCENTRATE** OR ANYTHING.
DON'T BE SO DRAMATIC.
I JUST FINISHED FLIGHT PRACTICE-- NOW **THAT'S** DANGEROUS.
BOO!
ACK!
DROP
MADE YA JUMP.
HEY! NO ROUGHHOUSING!

BLIP!
WHAAAAAAT DO YOU WANT, MAGGIE? I'M BUSY.
OH, UH, SORRY CLARICE.
WHAT'S WRONG?
WE KNOW WHAT YOU ARE

"WE KNOW WHAT YOU ARE"?
WHAT IS THIS?
NEWT? OI, NEWT!
WHAAAAAT?
ARE YOU FOOLING WITH THE COMPUTERS AGAIN?
NO, I'M PLAYING CASTLE CRUSHER 3000.
tap tap
_UNKNOWN
WE KNOW WHAT YOU ARE
WHAT DO YOU MEAN?
WE CAN SEE YOU, MONSTERS.
WHO ARE Y_
tap tap
I... I THINK...
_UNKNOWN
BLIP!
BLIP!

OMAR!!
SOMEONE CAN SEE US!
SLAP!
WHAT?!
SOMEONE IS TAKING PICTURES OF US WITH THE WEBCAM!
MAGGIE, GO GET AN AGENT, NOW.
O-OKAY!
SCAMPER
STAY CALM--
THEY'LL KNOW WHAT TO DO.
fwip

WHAT HAPPENED?
WE GOT A MESSAGE ON THE COMPUTER? LIKE A CHAT PROGRAM OR SOMETHING.
THEY SAID "WE KNOW WHAT YOU ARE." AND SAID THEY COULD SEE US!
I THOUGHT IT WAS NEWT HACKING THE SYSTEM AGAIN--
IT **WASN'T ME** THIS TIME!
I DON'T KNOW IF THEY CAN HEAR US...
...OOORRRR...
WE'LL REPLACE THESE. IT'S PROBABLY A BUG.
?!
HANG ON A--
G'NIGHT, KIDS.

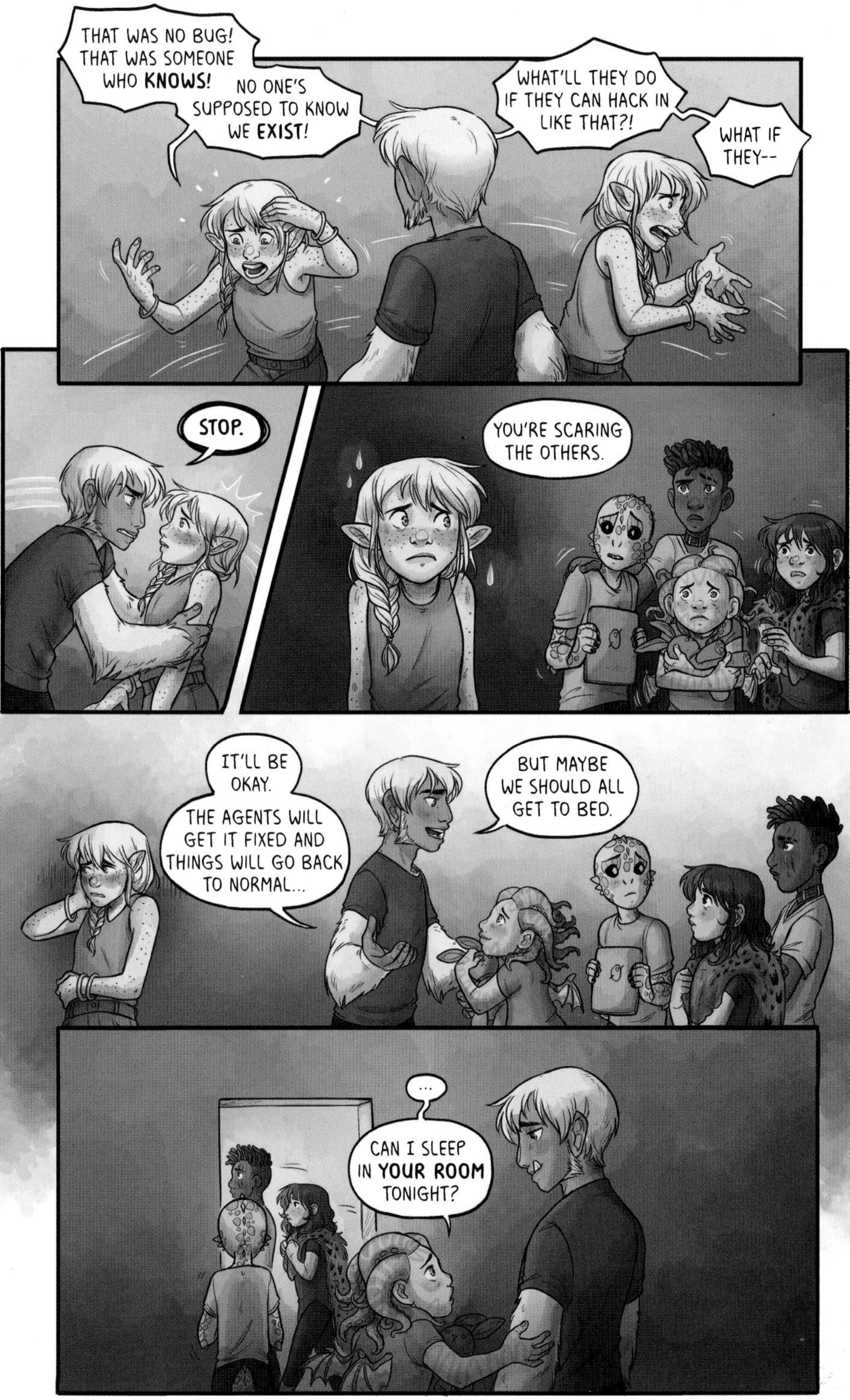
THAT WAS NO BUG! THAT WAS SOMEONE WHO **KNOWS!**
NO ONE'S SUPPOSED TO KNOW WE **EXIST!**
WHAT'LL THEY DO IF THEY CAN HACK IN LIKE THAT?!
WHAT IF THEY--
STOP.
YOU'RE SCARING THE OTHERS.
IT'LL BE OKAY.
THE AGENTS WILL GET IT FIXED AND THINGS WILL GO BACK TO NORMAL...
BUT MAYBE WE SHOULD ALL GET TO BED.
...
CAN I SLEEP IN **YOUR ROOM** TONIGHT?

knock knock knock
SYLVIE, IT'S THE MIDDLE OF THE NIGHT.
YEAH, AND SINCE THE BABIES ARE ASLEEP, WE CAN ACTUALLY TALK.
YOU'RE STILL FREAKED OUT?
OF COURSE I AM!
HOW COULD SOMEONE HACK INTO THE COMPUTERS OF A SECRET GOVERNMENT FACILITY--
FROM THE OUTSIDE??
THIS PLACE IS COMPLETELY OFF THE GRID--
IT'S SUPPOSED TO BE SECURE. THEY TOLD US WE'D BE SAFE HERE!
CALM DOWN. IT COULD BE SOME IDIOT ON THEIR LAPTOP A THOUSAND MILES AWAY.
BUT WHAT IF IT ISN'T? WHAT THEN?
I DON'T KNOW. BUT RIGHT NOW THE AGENTS ARE PROTECTING US.
PROTECTING US?
THEY KEEP US LOCKED AWAY IN THIS FANCY BOX, THE SAME THING DAY AFTER DAY, AND EXPECT US TO SAY THANK YOU SO MUCH, MAY I HAVE SOME MORE CARDBOARD FOOD, PLEASE?!
BETTER LOCKED IN HERE THAN OUT WITH THE NORMALS, ISN'T IT?
NO.
NO, IT ISN'T. IF SOMEONE CAN HACK THE SYSTEM, WHO'S TO SAY THEY CAN'T HACK THE LOCKS?

I'VE HAD ENOUGH OF CAGES. YOU DON'T UNDERSTAND.
SYLVIE...
WANT TO MEET SOME OF THE MOST SUPERSTITIOUS FOLKS ON THE PLANET? GO TALK TO THE IRISH.
I WAS A FOUNDLING, RIGHT? A COUPLE OF DAYS OLD, THEY FIND ME WAILING MY HEAD OFF OUT IN SOME FARMER'S FIELD.
MY EARS ARE A DEAD GIVEAWAY, OF COURSE, BUT THEY SUSPECTED RIGHT FROM THE START WHAT I WAS.
YOU DON'T EXACTLY FIND HUMAN BABIES IN THE MIDDLE OF A FAIRY RING.
THEY GAVE ME TO THIS HOME FOR OTHER ORPHANED OR ABANDONED KIDS. IT WAS FINE, AT THE START.
THEY'D ALWAYS PICK ON ME, THE POINTY-EARED GIRL. CALL ME ELF OR TROLL BABY AND SUCH.
I ALWAYS THOUGHT IT WAS LIKE MY FRECKLES. JUST SOMETHING I WAS BORN WITH AND COULDN'T HELP.
BUT THE MATRONS ALWAYS LOOKED LIKE THEY WERE WAITING... WAITING FOR ME TO GROW FANGS OR START EATING MICE OR SOME OTHER NONSENSE.

WHEN I WAS AROUND NINE, WE WERE OUT PLAYING BY A CREEK.
JOHN, THE ELDEST BOY, DECIDED IT'D BE FUNNY TO "SEE IF THE FAIRY BABY COULD FLY."
TURNS OUT, I **COULD.**
GASP!
SPLASH!
THEY DRAGGED ME BACK AND TOLD THE MATRONS I WAS A **DEMON,** SOME DEVIL OF THE TAIGA WHO WOULD CURSE US ALL.
I TRIED TO TELL THEM IT WAS AN ACCIDENT-- THAT I COULDN'T HELP IT.
THE MATRONS LOCKED ME IN THE CELLAR EACH TIME I SHOWED MY TRUE SELF.
THEY TOLD ME IT WAS FOR MY OWN GOOD, THAT I NEEDED THE DEMON SHUT OUT OF ME.
IT WAS SO DARK IN THERE.
RICE

WHEN THEY DID LET ME OUT, THE OTHER KIDS ACTED TERRIFIED OF ME.
ALL I'D DONE WAS HOVER THREE FEET OFF THE GROUND AND GLOW A LITTLE!
BUT WHEN THE MATRONS WEREN'T LOOKING, THEY CHANGED.
THEY BECAME THE DEMONS. AND I COULDN'T GET AWAY. WHERE WAS I SUPPOSED TO GO?
I HAD TO FIGHT BACK JUST TO MAKE IT STOP. BUT EVERY TIME I DID, IT WAS BACK TO THE CELLAR.
JOHN WAS THE WORST OF THEM. HE WOULD CATCH RATS AND TOSS THEM THROUGH THE CELLAR WINDOW. WATCH ME RUN AWAY.
ONE DAY... HE STOLE THE KEYS AND CAME TO FIND ME.

SYLVIE... I'M SO SORRY.
...THANKS.
UNTIL THEN I THOUGHT MY POWERS WERE JUST FLYING AND GLOWING.
LIKE I WAS SOME PRETTY PAPER LANTERN.
BUT WHEN HE TRIED TO TOUCH ME...
I FOUND OUT I HAD SOMETHING ELSE TOO.
YOU WANT TO LET GO OF ME.
YOU ARE FOUL.
YOU ARE NOTHING!
YOU WILL NEVER TOUCH ME AGAIN!

WHAT DID YOU DO TO HIM?
I... I HAVE A SORT OF... HYPNOSIS ABILITY? I CAN MAKE PEOPLE SEE THINGS... BELIEVE THEM COMPLETELY.
I CONVINCED HIM THAT THE WORLD WOULDN'T MISS HIM. IT... KIND OF BROKE HIS HEAD.
I DIDN'T MEAN TO--I WAS DEFENDING MYSELF! BUT THIS... OTHER SYLVIE SORT OF TOOK OVER.
BUT THEN THE MATRONS CAME AND SAW ME STANDING OVER HIM LIKE THAT...
IT WAS LIKE EVERYTHING THEY HAD ALWAYS FEARED ABOUT ME HAD SUDDENLY COME TRUE.
THEY CALLED THE GARDA--
THE WHAT?
OH, THE POLICE.
I SUPPOSE THEY DIDN'T KNOW WHAT ELSE TO DO. AFTER I TRIED TO EXPLAIN MY POWERS, THEY REALIZED THEY DIDN'T KNOW WHAT THEY WERE DEALING WITH.
SO THEY CALLED THE AMERICANS...
...AND I WAS BROUGHT HERE.

DO THE AGENTS KNOW ABOUT THIS... **ABILITY** OF YOURS?
YES. THAT'S WHAT THESE **BANGLES** ARE FOR.
THEY TOLD ME IT'S SOME KIND OF **ELECTROMAGNETIC PULSE**? IT KEEPS THE OTHER SYLVIE QUIET BUT STILL LETS ME FLY AND ALL THAT.
CAN'T USE THE HYPNOSIS THING WITH THEM ON... NOT THAT I'D **WANT** TO.
I'VE NEVER TOLD THE OTHERS ABOUT THIS. I... I DON'T WANT THEM TO KNOW.
THE OTHER ME IS... **NOT** A NICE PERSON.
THIS IS WHAT I MEAN, OMAR. I DON'T EVER WANT TO BE **LOCKED UP AND TORTURED** AGAIN.
AND I DON'T WANT TO HAVE TO DO **WHAT I DID** EVER AGAIN EITHER.
I JUST WANT A PLACE TO BE **SAFE**. I THOUGHT THIS WAS IT, BUT NOW I'M NOT SO SURE.
THANK YOU FOR TELLING ME. FOR TRUSTING ME.
WE'RE ALL IN THIS TOGETHER...

AND BESIDES...
THERE'S NO WAY THEY COULD BE WATCHING US RIGHT NOW,
RIGHT?

CHAPTER TWO

YOU CAN RUN BUT YOU CAN'T HIDE

MONDAY
TUESDAY
WEDNESDAY
THURSDAY
BLIP
BLEEP
nudge
? ? ?
SHRUG

I THINK THEY'RE WORRIED.
YEAH... I WAS GETTING THAT IMPRESSION TOO.

SO ARE YOU GOING TO TELL US WHAT'S HAPPENING,
OR ARE YOU JUST GOING TO STAND THERE STARING AT US?
shove
WHAT ARE YOU TALKING ABOUT, SYLVIE?
"WHAT AM I TALKING ABOUT!" YEAH GOOD ONE--
THERE'S JUST DOUBLE DUTY AGENTS AND WE'RE WATCHED EVERY MOMENT FOR NO REASON?
WHAT'S HAPPENING WITH THE COMPUTERS?!
YOU'VE REPLACED THEM WITH WAY NEWER ONES BUT YOU'RE ALL SO TENSE I FEEL LIKE I'M, GONNA EXPLODE!
THEY'RE JUST MAKING SURE EVERYTHING IS OKA--
WELL, IT'S MAKING ME PULL MY HAIR OUT!
SLAM
Y'KNOW WHAT?
I'M GOING TO BED.
ENJOY YOUR CARDBOARD NUGGETS WITH A SIDE OF "DON'T TELL US ANYTHING."
SHE DIDN'T EAT AT ALL...

SLAM!
BLOODY RIDICULOUS.
KEEPING US IN THE DARK...
fwip
WHISPERING BEHIND OUR BACKS LIKE THIS...
MAKING A FUSS...

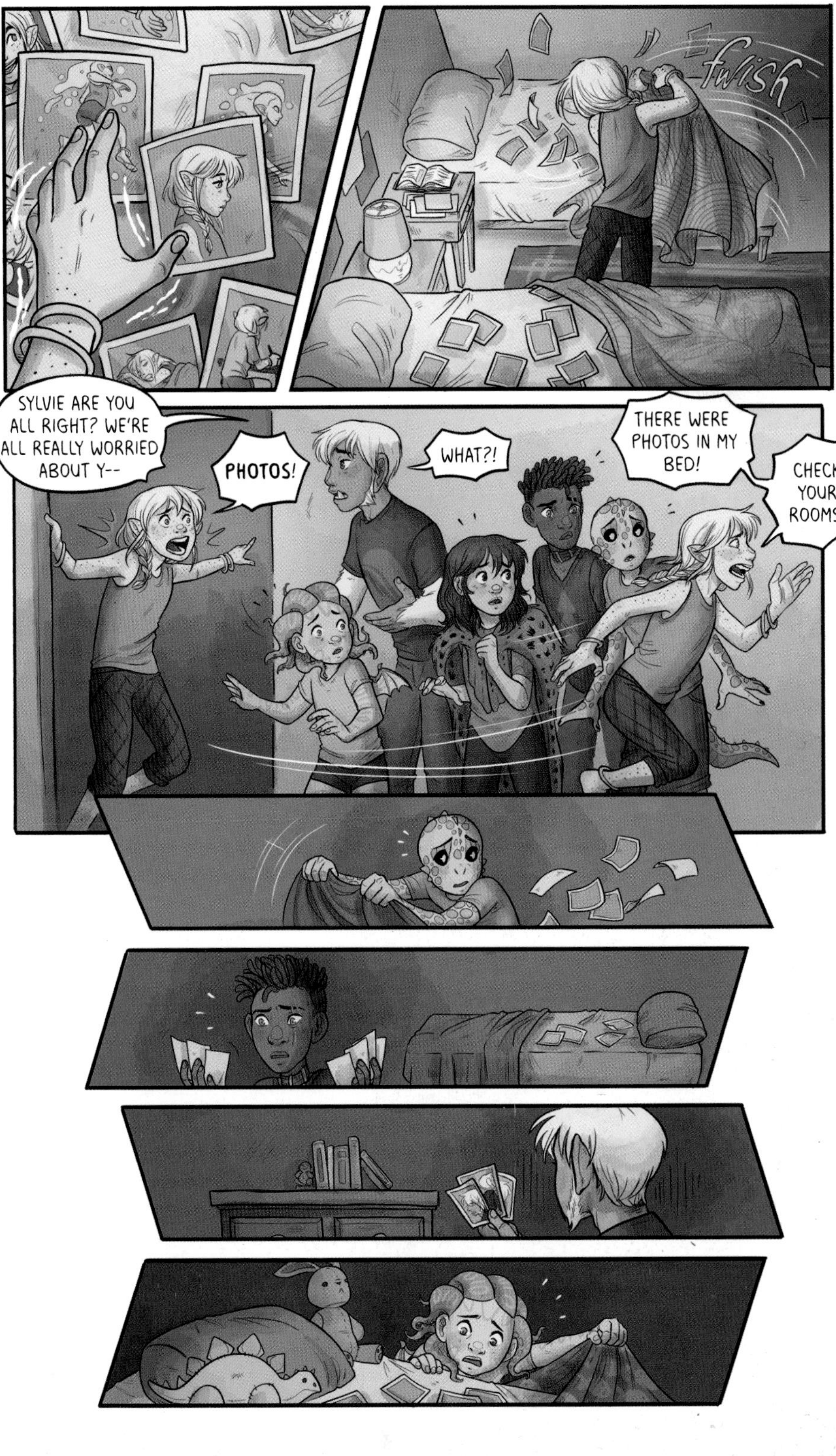
fwish
SYLVIE ARE YOU ALL RIGHT? WE'RE ALL REALLY WORRIED ABOUT Y--
PHOTOS!
WHAT?!
THERE WERE PHOTOS IN MY BED!
CHECK YOUR ROOMS!

WE'VE CORDONED OFF YOUR BEDROOMS AND ARE MAKING A **FULL INVESTIGATION.**
YOU'RE GOING TO BE SLEEPING HERE FOR THE NIGHT, SO GET COMFORTABLE.
LIGHTS OUT IN TEN MINUTES.
...AGENT RAMIREZ?
ARE WE... ARE WE SAFE HERE?
. . . . . .
LIGHTS OUT IN TEN, SYLVIE.
HEY!
IT'S LIKE A SLUMBER PARTY!
YEAH, ONLY WITH **ARMED GUARDS** OUTSIDE THE DOOR AND PEOPLE **BREAKING INTO OUR BEDROOMS.**
LIGHTS OUT, KIDS!
YEAH... ONLY WITH THAT...

ANYONE AWAKE?
WE'RE SUPPOSED TO BE SLEEPING.
I KNOW BUT I CAN'T SLEEP...
ME NEITHER.
IT'S FREAKY, ISN'T IT? SOMEONE BREAKING INTO THE FACILITY... GETTING IN OUR ROOMS, AND NONE OF THE AGENTS NOTICED?
YEAH...
OH MY GOOD GOD, CAN WE NOT TALK ABOUT IT WHILE THERE ARE NO LIGHTS ON??
TURN ON A LIGHT IF YOU'RE SCARED, SYLVIE.
I AM NOT GETTING IN TROUBLE WHILE THE AGENTS ARE THIS ON EDGE, THANKYOUVERYMUCH!
THEN QUIT COMPLAINING!
SHH!
YOU SHHH!
DON'T TELL US WHAT TO DO!
IF YOU ALL WAKE MAGGIE UP SHE'S GOING TO KEEP US AWAKE ALL NIGHT. EVERYONE GO TO SLEEP.
...FINE.
FINE.
...GOD, MAGGIE SNORES SO LOUD.
GO TO BED!

RISE AND SHINE, GANG! BIG NEWS!
CLICK!
IT HAS BEEN DECIDED THAT DUE TO THE RECENT SECURITY BREACHES, YOU'RE BEING **RELOCATED** TODAY!
WE'RE **MOVING**??
YUP! AS SOON AS POSSIBLE.
GUHHHH...
THESE ARE FOR YOU TO PACK YOUR ESSENTIALS.
YOU'LL NEED YOUR TOOTHBRUSHES AND AT LEAST ONE CHANGE OF CLOTHES.
EVERYTHING ELSE WILL BE BROUGHT TO THE NEW FACILITY LATER.
WHERE EXACTLY ARE WE GOING?
THAT'S **CLASSIFIED**, NEWT. BUT REST ASSURED IT'S MORE SECURE THAN THIS FACILITY.
CLAP CLAP!
NOW, HOP TO IT!
LOOKS LIKE MAGGIE HAS THE RIGHT IDEA!

WHAT ARE YOU DOING?
GOTTA MAKE SURE ALL MY STUFFIES FIT!
DID YOU PACK YOUR TOOTHBRUSH?
OH... OOPS.
THAT'S OKAY, I'VE GOT IT HERE. YOU'RE PRETTY EXCITED, HUH?
YUP!! I'VE ONLY BEEN OUTSIDE ONCE BEFORE!
AND I DON'T REALLY REMEMBER IT... BUT I BET IT WAS GREAT!
DO YOU THINK THERE'LL BE TREES AT THE NEW PLAYROOM?
MAYBE WE CAN PLAY OUTSIDE THERE!
DO YOU THINK THERE'LL BE OTHER KIDS AT THE NEW PLACE?
MAYBE WE'LL GET OUR OWN ROOMS!
THIS ROOM SMELLS TOO MUCH LIKE LIZARD.
HEYYY!
sigh
YOU'VE ONLY BEEN HERE A MONTH AND WE'RE MOVING ALREADY, HUH?
tuck
zzzZiiip!
WELL...
THE NEW PLACE WILL SURE BE BETTER THAN THIS ONE.

NICE HAT.
-SNERK-
I AM NOT GETTING SUNBURNED ON MY FIRST DAY OUT.
EVERYONE PACKED?
YEEEES!
THESE ARE FOR YOU.
WHAT ARE THOSE?
SHOES.
SHOES?!
YOU HAVE TO WEAR THEM.
I'M NOT WEARING ANY SHOES!
THE TARMAC IS HOT. YOU'LL BURN YOUR FEET.
YOU'LL BURN YOUR FEET!
MAGGIE, PUT ON THE SHOES.
I DON'T WANNA!
GLARE
FINE!

STOMP
STOMP
PFF
THIS WAY, KIDS!
WHOA!! WE'RE RIDING IN **THAT**?!
WAY BETTER THAN WALKING!
EVERYONE ALL SET? SEAT BELTS, PLEASE!
THIS IS SO COOL!
MOVE OVER.
WOW!

VRRRRRRRRR
WHERE'S THE CONVOY?
THEY'LL CATCH UP.
SHOULDN'T WE WAIT FOR THEM?
DON'T WORRY ABOUT IT. NO ONE'S OUT HERE.
?
I FORGOT THE DESERT WAS SO PRETTY.
YEAH, IT'S PRETTY BECAUSE WE HAVE AIR CONDITIONING!
LOOK! A CACTUS!
RR
RRR
LOOK! ANOTHER CACTUS!

HOLA
NOW LEAVING
RESTRICTED AREA

WHO ARE ALL OF THESE GUYS?
NO ENTRY

OH, THEY'RE JUST A BUNCH OF WEIRDOS.
THEY THINK THE GOVERNMENT IS HIDING **ALIENS** AND **MONSTERS** OUT HERE!
BUT...
DO YOU THINK THEY COULD HAVE BEEN THE ONES WHO HACKED INTO THE FACILITY?
THERE'S NO WAY.
THE FIREWALLS AND SECURITIES ARE TOO STRONG FOR PEOPLE LIKE THIS. THEY WOULD HAVE NEEDED **INSIDE** HELP.
BYE, BUNCH OF WEIRDOS!!
I HOPE YOU FIND THE **ALIENS**!!
F.R.E.A.K.I.S.H
HEY!!
WHOOPS-- SORRY, NEWT, I **FORGOT**.
YOU **FORGOT** THAT I'M AN **ALIEN**?!

♫SOOO...♪
ARE WE THERE YET?
...HOW BOUT NOW?
MAGGIE, **SHUT UP**!!
WHY ARE WE TURNING OFF THE ROAD?

WHERE ARE YOU HEADING? I DIDN'T GET ANY ORDERS THAT WE WERE LEAVING THE ROAD.
I WAS BRIEFED RIGHT BEFORE WE LEFT.
ADDITIONAL SECURITY MEASURE.
I THINK I WOULD HAVE HEARD SOMETHING ABOUT THIS.
IF YOU WEREN'T INFORMED, THEY MUST HAVE HAD A REASON TO **MISTRUST** YOU.
MISTRUST **ME**??
I'M NOT THE ONE TAKING A CAR FULL OF **CHILDREN** AWAY FROM THE SAFE ROAD--
THEY ARE **IRREGULARITIES.**
NOT CHILDREN.
NEWT. NEWT, YOU NEED TO WAKE UP.
RIGHT NOW.
HUH... WHA?

AGENT CLARK, WHO BRIEFED YOU ON THIS DETOUR?
THE COMMANDER, OBVIOUSLY.
THEN THE COMMANDER SHOULD BE ABLE TO CONFIRM AND SEND ME OUR NEXT COORDINATES,
SHOULDN'T HE?
CLACK
LUNGE!
swerve
GASP!
ACK!

WHAT DO YOU THINK YOU'RE **DOING**??
AGENT CLARK, PULL OVER THE VEHICLE.
NO.
PULL OVER THIS CAR, ***NOW!!!***
WHERE ARE YOU TAKING US, AGENT CLARK?
WHO ARE YOU?!
WHY ARE YOU DOING THIS?!
WHAT'S GOING ON??

PULL OVER THE CAR, OR I WILL DO IT FOR YOU.
NO. I HAVE TO DO THIS.
I HAVE TO DO THIS...
OR HE'LL KILL ME.
YOU'RE THE ONE WHO HACKED INTO THE FACILITY, AREN'T YOU?
YOU SAID IT YOURSELF, THE SECURITIES WERE TOO POWERFUL FOR SOMEONE ON THE OUTSIDE. YOU WERE THE ONE WHO SUGGESTED MOVING THEM--
THE COMMANDER DIDN'T SEND YOU ORDERS, DID HE.
CLICK
WHO ARE YOU WORKING FOR?!
SLAM

WHAT NOW, CLARK? WHERE ARE YOU TAKING US?
YOU'LL KNOW WHEN WE GET THERE.
IS HE GOING TO KILL US??
hhnng...
NO. WE'RE TOO **VALUABLE**.
BUT WE'VE GOT TO GET OUT OF HERE.
OH MY GOD, OH MY GOD, OH MY GOD.
SYLVIE, YOU HAVE TO SAVE US.
W- WHAT??
NO TALKING!!
jump!
YOU'RE THE ONLY ONE WHO CAN DO IT. I CAN'T REACH HIM FROM BACK HERE.
OMAR, I **C-CAN'T**.
YOU HAVE TO USE YOUR POWER.
SAVE US, SYLVIE...
PLEASE.

slip
tremble
gasp
haaaaaaaoooohhh finally!

agent claaaaark...
I SAID NO TALK--
sssshhhhhh...
WHAT THE HELL ARE YOU DOING?!
OH, SHUSH NOW...
YOU REALLY NEED TO KEEP A BETTER EYE ON THE ROAD, AGENT CLARK.
CAN'T YOU SEE IT??

. . . you're driving us right off the
edge of a cliff . . . aren't you?

ha ha!
ha ha ha ha ha ha h
SWERVE
ahhh ha ha ha ha ha haaaaaa
screeeeeeech
SLAM
KA

ahhh ha ha ha ha!
ha ha ha ha!
tck
tck
tck
tck

CHAPTER THREE

WHITEOUT

KA-KRASH!!!
NANI?? YOU OKAY?
I'M ALL RIGHT!

WHAT ARE YOU DOING?
I WAS LOOKING FOR AN OLD PHOTO OF YOUR PARENTS.
BUT MY **KNEES** WERE ACTING UP AGAIN AND I DROPPED THE DAMN THING.
GIVE ME A HAND, WOULD YOU?
shff
sff
AH! FOUND IT!

OH, I HAVEN'T SEEN THAT ONE.
THEY LOOK SO HAPPY.
THEY WERE HAPPY PEOPLE.
HERE, LOVE, WHY DON'T YOU PUT IT WITH THE OTHERS?
ALL RIGHT.

X02-914
WEISZ, REBECCA
DENVER, COL
UNITED STATES
KATHMANDU
NEPAL
We the People
PASSPORT
PASSEPORT
PASAPORTE
USA
UNITED STATES OF AMERICA
WEISZ
REBECCA
UNITED STATES OF AMERICA
USA
AGH, WHAT A MESS... I'LL CLEAN IT UP AFTER BREAKFAST.
I'LL DO IT FOR YOU IF YOU WANT TO START COOKING.

LOCAL CLIMBERS MISSING
स्थानीय आरोहीहरू हराइए
OH, THANK YOU, OMAR. WHAT DO YOU WANT TO EAT?
I COULD BOTHER THE NEIGHBOR FOR SOME EGGS IF YOU LIKE.
AND WE ALWAYS HAVE RICE.
COULD PUT TOGETHER SOME LEFTOVER CURRY MAYBE?
...OMAR?

ARE YOU ALL RIGHT, DEAR?
OH, YEAH I'M OKAY JUST...
THINKING ABOUT THEM.
THINKING ABOUT WHAT THEY WERE LIKE. I BARELY REMEMBER THEM.
SOMETIMES I WONDER WHAT THEY WOULD DO IF THEY WERE HERE.
THEY WERE **WONDERFUL,** OMAR.
JUST LIKE **YOU**.

OOF!
WATCH IT, KID!
S-SORRY!!
OMAR! HIDE YOUR **TEETH**!
HEY, WHAT'S UP WITH YOUR--
OH, SO SORRY, SIR! YOU ARE **MIKARU**, YES?
WE'RE WHAT?
SHE MEANS CLIMBERS.
OH YEAH.
MIKARU NEVER COME INTO THE VILLAGE. WHAT A SURPRISE! SHOULDN'T YOU BE AT BASE CAMP, IF THE CLIMB STARTS TOMORROW?
WE WANTED TO SEE THE SIGHTS BEFORE WE SET OUT.

WELL, ENJOY THE SIGHTS, BUT YOU SHOULD HEAD BACK SOON. BAD WEATHER TONIGHT!
PUSH
PUSH
HEY! WAIT!
WHAT ARE YOU DOING?
SOMETHING'S **WEIRD** ABOUT THAT KID!
HURRY, OMAR. LET'S GO!
HEY! HEY, LADY. **STOP**!
LEAVE US ALONE!!
LET ME LOOK AT--
HEY!
HOLY SH-- **I KNEW IT**!
WHAT IS THAT **THING**?!

THAT'S A YETI!
THAT'S A BABY YETI, AND SHE'S KEEPING IT AS A PET!
WE HAVE TO CALL SOMEONE!
HOW DARE YOU!
HOW DARE YOU ASSAULT MY GRANDSON!
GET OUT OF OUR VILLAGE!
NEVER COME BACK!
UFF!
shove
SLAM!
I CAN'T BELIEVE THAT JUST HAPPENED. A YETI!
WE HAVE TO TELL THE AUTHORITIES--THAT MONSTER COULD
HURT SOMEONE!

NANI... WHAT ARE WE GONNA DO?
WHAT?
WHAT ARE WE GONNA DO ABOUT **ME**?
WHAT IF I END UP LOOKING JUST LIKE **DAD**?
EVERY OUTSIDER IS **AFRAID** OF ME, AND IT'S JUST GOING TO GET **WORSE!**
THEY ALL THINK I'M A **MONSTER**, NANI.
ARE YOU?
W-WHAT??
ARE YOU A MONSTER?
I... I DON'T THINK SO??
IT CAN'T BE THAT **SIMPLE**!
YES, IT **CAN**.
IT'S UP TO YOU TO DETERMINE WHAT KIND OF PERSON **YOU WANT TO BE**.
THOSE WHO JUDGE YOU BY **APPEARANCE**, WITHOUT EVEN TAKING THE TIME TO **KNOW** YOU,
DON'T GET TO DECIDE YOU'RE A **MONSTER**.

BUT...
BUT...
I'M HALF YETI, NANI! I'M BARELY EVEN HUMAN!
DOES THAT MATTER??
YES!
NO??
I DON'T KNOW!
OMAR.
LISTEN TO ME.
WE MAY NOT SHARE THE SAME BLOOD, BUT WE ARE FAMILY. YOU ARE MY GRANDSON.
I LOVED YOUR PARENTS LIKE THEY WERE MY OWN, AND THEY LOVED YOU MORE THAN ANYTHING IN THE WORLD.
FOOLISH PEOPLE WILL ALWAYS BE AFRAID OF THOSE WHO ARE DIFFERENT, BUT YOUR DIFFERENCES DON'T MAKE YOU WRONG.
THEIR OPINIONS BE DAMNED. I LOVE YOU. EVERYONE IN THIS VILLAGE LOVES YOU.
AND NOTHING THOSE IDIOTS SAY WILL EVER CHANGE THAT.
I LOVE YOU TOO.
THANK YOU.

BUT... NANI, WHAT IF THEY COME BA--
KNOCK KNOCK
WHO ON EARTH??
WHAT DO YOU WANT?
THERE!
THERE IT IS!
OUT OF THE WAY!
CRACK
HEY!!
GET YOUR HANDS OFF HER!
OMAR, NO!

strike strike
STOP, WOMAN!
NO!! NOT MY OMAR! LET ME GO! LET ME GO!
WHAM
NO!
GRAAAAAAGHH!

ARGH
SLAM
CATCH HIM!!
NANI--
...MY OMAR...
CRACK!
AH!
NO--NANI, WAIT!

WHERE AM I?
THIS IS YOUR NEW HOME. A PLACE FOR IRREGULARITIES.
LIKE YOU.
IRREGULARITIES?
THIS IS FOR YOUR SAFETY, AND FOR THE SAFETY OF **NORMAL PEOPLE.**
NORMAL PEOPLE...
...YETI... AN OLD WOMAN WAS **KILLED**...
...BETTER HE'S IN HERE FOR... ...**SAFETY**...
YOU NEED TO LEARN TO CONTROL YOUR STRENGTH, OR YOU MIGHT **HURT** SOMEONE.
I KNOW.
OMAR, MEET MAGGIE. SHE'S THE OTHER IRREGULARITY IN THE FACILITY.
O-MAR...
SHE'S...
SO TINY...
BRBBBLBRBBL
OMAR...
OMAR!
OMAR!!

OMAR! ARE YOU OKAY??
AHH... MY HEAD...
M...MAGGIE?
SNIFF
I'M SO GLAD YOU'RE OKAY!!
I WAS SO WORRIED ABOUT YOU--ALSO WE CRASHED THE CAR.
WHICH WAS KINDA COOL BUT ALSO SO SCARY. ARE YOU SURE YOU'RE OKAY?!
I'M FINE, PIPSQUEAK, I'M FINE.

HOW LONG WAS I OUT?
IS EVERYONE ALL RIGHT?
NOT LONG. MAYBE TEN MINUTES? YOU HIT YOUR HEAD PRETTY GOOD.
YEAH, I REALLY DID.
WE'RE ALL OKAY. THE CRASH COULD HAVE BEEN A LOT WORSE.
JAALI HAS A SKINNED KNEE.
AND I THINK CLARICE TWISTED HER WRIST.
AND SYLVIE...
SYLVIE DOESN'T WANT TO TALK TO ANYONE RIGHT NOW.

I'M GONNA TRY TO TALK TO HER.
OMAR?
HM?
...WHO IS **NANI**?
W-WHAT?
WHEN YOU WERE KNOCKED OUT, YOU KEPT SAYING NANI, NANI. WHO'S THAT?
NANI IS... A SHERPA WORD FOR **GRANDMA**.
OH, DID YOU HAVE A DREAM ABOUT YOUR GRANDMA?
WHERE IS SHE NOW?
IS SHE NICE?
SHE'S... SHE'S GONE, MAGGIE. A LONG TIME AGO.
OHH...
HEY, STAY HERE A MINUTE, ALL RIGHT?
WHY?
I NEED TO GO TALK TO SYLVIE. SHE'S BEEN THROUGH A LOT AND NEEDS HELP RIGHT NOW.
CAN I HELP TOO?
IN... IN A MINUTE, YEAH. I'LL BE RIGHT BACK.
OKAY.

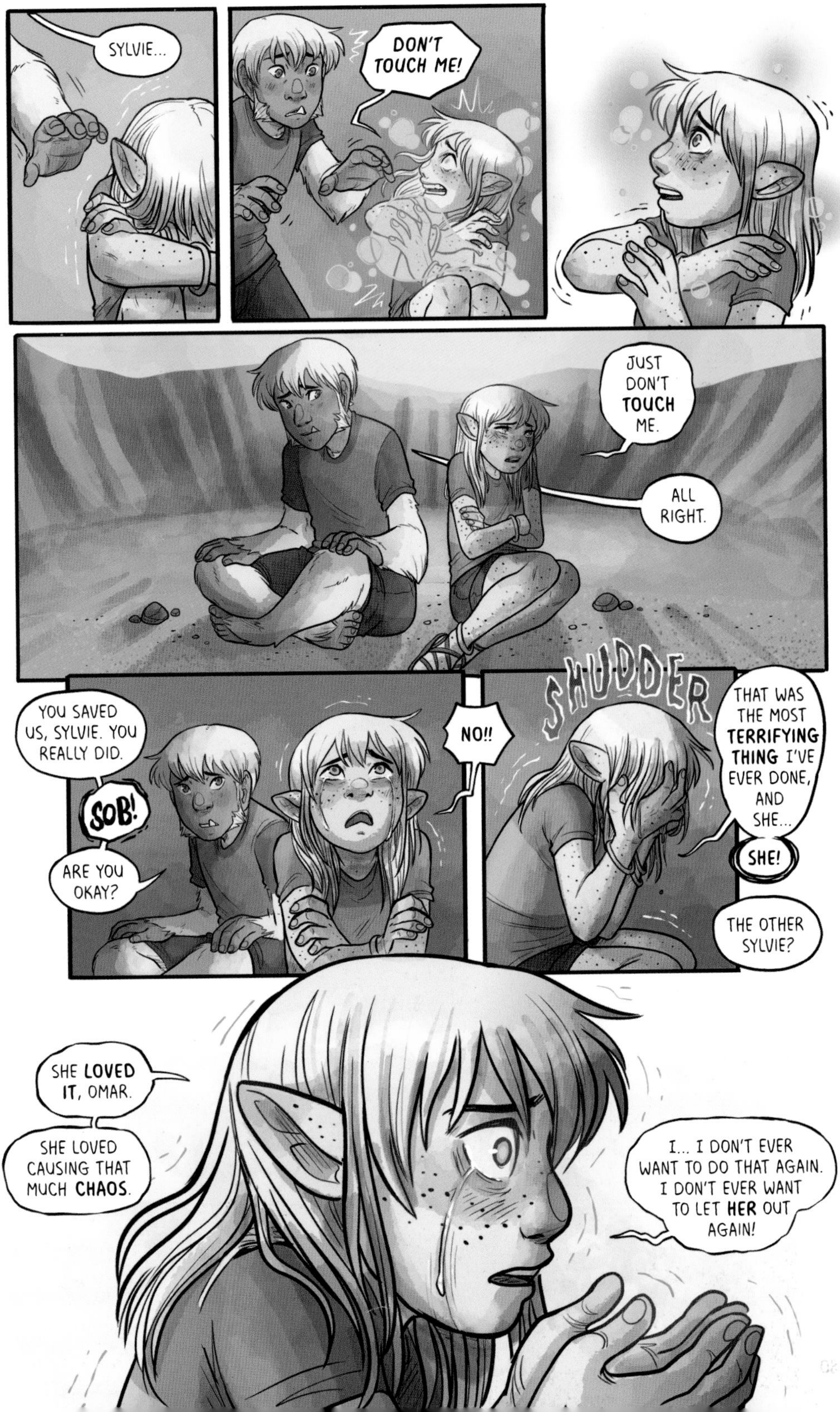
SYLVIE...
DON'T TOUCH ME!
JUST DON'T TOUCH ME.
ALL RIGHT.
YOU SAVED US, SYLVIE. YOU REALLY DID.
SOB!
ARE YOU OKAY?
NO!!
SHUDDER
THAT WAS THE MOST TERRIFYING THING I'VE EVER DONE, AND SHE...
SHE!
THE OTHER SYLVIE?
SHE LOVED IT, OMAR.
SHE LOVED CAUSING THAT MUCH CHAOS.
I... I DON'T EVER WANT TO DO THAT AGAIN. I DON'T EVER WANT TO LET HER OUT AGAIN!

I THINK... YOU MIGHT **HAVE TO** SOMEDAY.
TCH! THAT'S RUBBISH ADVICE, THANKS A LOT!
I MEAN...
ALL OF US HAVE **SOME** KIND OF **MONSTER** IN US, SYLVIE.
YOU'VE JUST GOT... A PARTICULARLY DIFFICULT ONE.
AND WE DON'T KNOW WHAT'S AHEAD OF US.
YOUR ABILITIES ARE **INCREDIBLE**, EVEN IF THEY'RE SCARY.
AND IF I'M BEING HONEST--
IF ANYONE CAN CONTROL A MONSTER LIKE THAT--
IT'S **YOU.**
YOU'RE THE SNARKIEST, SCARIEST, MOST BADASS PERSON I'VE EVER MET.
YOU IDIOT.
-SNIFF-
OF **COURSE** I AM.
BUT I'M NOT DOING THAT AGAIN ANY TIME SOON.
NOT UNTIL... NOT UNTIL I'M READY.

NEWT--COULD YOU GET OUR BAGS OUT OF THE TRUCK?
WE NEED TO FIGURE OUT WHERE WE'RE GOING AND WHAT WE'RE GONNA DO NOW.
HEY, TINY.
OH... UHH.
THE... UH... THE **AGENTS** ARE STILL IN THERE?
SHE... UHM. AND HE... THEY **WEREN'T MOVING**, WE THINK THEY MIGHT BE... DEAD. SO WE DIDN'T...
I'LL GET THEM.
OH! THANKS, JAALI.
ANYWAY...
I FOUND THIS!
IT'S AGENT RAMIREZ'S **SATELLITE PHONE.**
I THINK I CAN GET SOME KIND OF **INTERNET CONNECTION** WITH IT.
HOOK IT UP TO MY O-PAD AND TRY TO FIND A WAY **OUT** OF THIS **DESERT**!
GOOD THINKING!

OKAY... IT LOOKS LIKE THERE'S A TOWN ABOUT FOURTEEN MILES AWAY.
FOURTEEN MILES?
WELL YEAH, SYLVIE, WE'RE PRACTICALLY IN THE MIDDLE OF NOWHERE.
I KNOW. THAT'S JUST... A LONG WAY TO WALK.
UNLESS YOU WANT TO GO BACK TO THE PLAYROOM, THIS IS OUR ONLY OPTION.
MAYBE FROM THIS TOWN WE COULD CATCH A BU--
GROAN
GASP!
CLARK!!
HE JUST MOVED!
WHAT?!
HE'S ALIVE?? AFTER ALL THAT?
YES!! WHAT ARE WE GONNA DO??

HE TRIED TO KILL US.
SO WHAT ARE YOU SAYING??
WE'RE SUPPOSED TO DO THE SAME TO HIM?
HE'D **DESERVE** IT.
HOW CAN YOU SAY THAT? WE CAN'T--WE COULDN'T... DO **THAT**!
STOP.
THIS IS STUPID.
HE'S BEEN THROUGH A CAR CRASH AND...
...WHAT I DID TO HIM. THAT'S ENOUGH.
THERE'S NO WAY HE'LL BE ABLE TO FOLLOW US, SO WE'RE JUST GOING TO LEAVE HIM HERE.
WITH AGENT RAMIREZ...GONE... I JUST DON'T WANT TO HURT ANYONE ELSE.
WE'RE NOT **THOSE KINDS** OF **MONSTERS**, RIGHT?
...

hop
ALL RIGHT THEN.
BUT AT LEAST...
FLING
...I'M GETTING RID OF THIS!

OKAY... THE R-ROAD SHOULD BE J-JUST UP AHEAD.
S-S-SEE! I KNEW WE'D FIND THE R-ROAD EVENTUALLY!
GOOD JOB, NEWT!
G-GOD, IT'S COLD. DID ANYONE BRING A B-BLANKET OR SOMETHING?
CHATTER
HEH.
W-W-**WHAT**??
NOTHING, IT'S JUST... YOU WOULD **DIE** IN NEPAL.
THIS IS LIKE... EARLY **SPRING** THERE.

OH, R-RIGHT, I FORGOT WE'RE T-TRAVELING WITH THE **ABOMINABLE SNOW BOY** HERE--
VVVRRRRRR
HIDE!!
VVRRRRRRRRRRRRRRRRRRR
F.R.E.A.K.I.S.H
F.R.E.A.K.I.S.H.com
I'M SQUATCHING -YOU-
AREA 51 SURVIVO
ARIZONA
1LUMNAT1
LOCH YES
MOTHMAN
WHY CAN'T WE GET A RIDE WITH **THEM?**
snerk

ARE YOU KIDDING ME?? THOSE ARE THE GUYS WHO WERE STALKING THE GATE--
THEY'D DO **EXPERIMENTS** ON US OR SOMETHING!
snort
WHAT IN THE WORLD ARE YOU LAUGHING AT? THEY ALMOST **SAW US**!
I'M SORRY, I CAN'T HELP IT!
WHAT IS SO FUNNY?!
PFFFFT
HEE HEE HEE
THEIR BUMPER STICKER SAID "I'M SQUATCHING YOU"!
HA HA HA HA HA HA HA HA HA HA HA HA HA HA HA HA HA HA
PFF
HEH.
HA HA HA HA HA HA HA HA HA HA HA HA HA HA
I DIDN'T KNOW YOU MADE ANY NOISE!! YOU CAN LAUGH! WOW!
. . . . . .
HA HA HA HA HA HA HA HA HA HA HA HA

HA HA HA HA HA
WE ARE IN **DANGER**,
IN THE MIDDLE OF THE **DESERT**, AND YOU'RE **LAUGHING**?!
HA HA HA HA HA HA HA HA
PFFT
HA HA HA HA HA HA HA HA HA HA HA HA HA HA HA HA HA HA HA HA HA HA HA HA HA HA HA HA HA HA HA HA HA HA HA HA HA HA HA HA HA
SIGH
LOOK AT THE **STARS**.

I NEVER KNEW THERE WERE SO MANY.

CHAPTER FOUR

HEAT WAVES

RISE AND SHINE!
UGHHHHHH...

THE EARLY BIRD GETS THE WORM!
OH, WAIT, IT'S THE **DESERT**. THERE'S NO WORMS...
THE EARLY BIRD GETS THE... UH... **BEETLE**!
MY TUMMY'S RUMBLING--
I'M HUNGRY!
ME TOO BUT WE DON'T HAVE ANYTHING NOW.
WE HAVE TO GET TO THE TOWN FIRST.
THEN WE CAN FIND SOMETHING TO EAT.
O...OMAR?
PIPSQUEAK? YOU OKAY?
I DON'T...
I DON'T FEEL SO GOOD.
MAGGIE, ARE YOU OKAY??
I THINK SHE'S CLOSE TO **HEATSTROKE**.
WHAT??
OOF
WUMP

WELL... SHE'S **AMPHIBIOUS**, RIGHT? HER BODY CAN'T PROCESS THE HEAT LIKE OURS.
SOMEONE SHOULD CARRY HER, AND WE SHOULD TRY TO GET HER OUT OF THE SUN.
HERE YOU GO, RUNT. SOME SHADE.
HEY, TINY.
MM?
DON'T FALL ASLEEP, OKAY?
I CAN'T.
WHY'S THAT?
YOU'RE ALL SWEATY AND GROSS.
HAH, SORRY.
KEEP TALKING TO ME, ALL RIGHT?
...YOU'RE STINKY TOO.
SWEATY YETI. HA HA.
MHMM.
GOOD ONE, TELL ME ANOTHER.
...IF IT WAS YOUR BIRTHDAY...
YOU'D BE A CONFETTI YETI.
GOOD, GOOD.
...IF YOU WANTED DINNER YOU'D HAVE SPAGHETTI YETI.
I LIKE SPAGHETTI.
...IF YOU HAD BROWN HAIR YOU'D BE A BRUNETTE-Y YETI.
THAT ONE WASN'T AS GOOD.
I KNOW.

MOTEL
ICE
105
CATCH!
SHH!
GO GO GO,
QUICK!
PHEW
CLICK
I CAN'T BELIEVE WE MADE IT. FOURTEEN MILES IS SO **FAR**!!
WHUMP

FSSSSH
HERE, TINY.
DON'T DRINK TOO FAST, OKAY?
gulp gulp
MHM.
HEY... ANYONE NEED THE BATHROOM OR CAN I GO?
NAH.
GO FOR IT.
SO...
WHAT ARE WE GOING TO DO NOW?

WE COULD ORDER ROOM SERVICE!
MENU
HAHA, YEAH RIGHT.
I AM HUNGRY THOUGH...
WE ALL ARE.
nod nod
MENU
I THINK I SAW SOME **VENDING MACHINES** OUTSIDE...
BUT WE DON'T HAVE ANY **MONEY**.
OH, UH... WHAT, CLARICE?
RUMMAGE
WHERE DID YOU GET THAT?!
$ $ $

SCRIBBLE
SCRIBBLE
SO YOU... YOU JUST TOOK HIS WALLET??
CLARICE THAT'S SO-- SO--!
SHRUG
SO BRILLIANT!!
HA! I KNEW YOU WERE MORE THAN YOU SEEMED!
RUFFLE

CLARICE, YOU'RE AMAZING!
CAN I HAVE CHIPS, PLEASE??
HOW MUCH MONEY IS IT??
sure was fun...
...wasn't it?
ha ha ha ha
ha ha ha ha

beep
beep
VRRRRRT
RRUUMBLE
RRUUMMBLE
GAS
EXCUSE ME, MA'AM, CAN WE ASK YOU A FEW QUESTIONS?
...
...
...
...MISSING KIDS?
NO... I HAVEN'T SEEN ANYTHING.
I'LL BE SURE TO KEEP AN EYE OUT THOUGH.
THANK YOU, MA'AM, WE DO SO APPRECIATE YOUR HELP.

I'M BACK.
FOOD!
OH MY GOSH, I LOVE THESE!!
CAN I HAVE THESE CAKES?
CLARICE, WHAT WOULD YOU LIKE?
DON'T HOG THE CHIPS!
HEY-- SAVE SOME FOR SYLVIE, OKAY?
CRONCH CRONCH
SAVE SOME WHAT FOR ME?
OH, HEY, SNACKS! BRILLIANT!
I'M STARVING!
...
WHAT?!
YOU LOOK REALLY PRETTY, SYLVIE!

HEY, CAN I TALK TO YOU BOTH FOR A SECOND?
WE NEED TO FIGURE OUT WHERE TO GO NEXT.
I SAW SOME AGENTS OUTSIDE.
MONCH MONCH
WHAT?!
SHH!!
WHAT ARE YOU TALKING ABOUT OVER THERE??
NOTHING! EVERYTHING'S FINE--
YUP! ALL GOOD HERE!
WE'VE GOT A PERFECT PLAN AND THERE ARE DEFINITELY NO AGENTS OUTSIDE, NONE AT ALL!
THERE ARE AGENTS OUTSIDE, AND NOW YOU'RE LYING TO US?!
HOW LONG HAVE YOU KNOWN ABOUT THIS??
heh heh...

OKAY, OKAY, LISTEN-- I JUST NOW SAW THEM WHILE I WAS GETTING FOOD, ALL RIGHT? CALM DOWN.
WERE YOU PLANNING TO **TELL** EVERYONE, OMAR??
ME AND SYLVIE AND JAALI WERE GONNA FIGURE IT OUT. I DIDN'T WANT YOU TO **PANIC**--
YOU CAN'T MAKE DECISIONS FOR THE WHOLE GROUP!
I'M THE OLDEST AND YOU ALL HAVE **ALWAYS** MADE ME DECIDE THINGS FOR YOU--
SO SYLVIE AND JAALI CAN KNOW BUT NOT THE REST OF US??
WE'RE **OLDER**! WE'RE SUPPOSED TO **PROTECT YOU!**
WE SHOULD ALL DECIDE **TOGETHER**!!
YEAH!
FINE! FINE. OKAY.
I SAW TWO TRUCKS FULL OF AGENTS AND THEY'RE OBVIOUSLY LOOKING FOR US.
WHAT DO **YOU** THINK WE SHOULD DO, NEWT?

WHY CAN'T WE GO TALK TO THE AGENTS? THEY CAN TAKE US BACK TO THE PLAYROOM AND FIGURE ALL OF THIS OUT.
NO.
WE CAN'T TRUST THE LOT OF THEM. WE TRUSTED **CLARK**, AND YOU SAW WHAT HE DID.
ANY OF THEM COULD TURN ON US.
I DON'T WANT TO GO BACK TO THE **DESERT**!
WE WON'T GO BACK TO THE DESERT. WE HAVE TO FIND SOMEWHERE ELSE.
YEAH, I SAW A **BUS STATION** TOO.
I DON'T THINK WE HAVE ENOUGH MONEY FOR BUS TICKETS...
...I COULD CALL **MY DAD.**
WHAT CAN YOUR DAD DO?
WELL... HE'S A BIG POLITICIAN AND STUFF. AND HE HAS A LOT OF MONEY.
SO HE COULD GET US TICKETS TO...
TO...?
WASHINGTON, D.C. THAT'S WHERE HE LIVES.
THAT'S A GREAT IDEA. CAN YOU CALL HIM?
YEAH...
YEAH. I'LL CALL HIM.
GIVE ME A MINUTE.

SYLVIE, I REALLY LIKE YOUR HAIR!
WHY'D YOU CUT IT?
CAN YOU CUT MINE?
SOOO...
OH, UH...
...THE BRAID WAS GETTING IN THE WAY. AND I NEEDED A **CHANGE**, Y'KNOW?
I DON'T THINK WE CAN CUT THROUGH YOURS, PIPSQUEAK.
RUFFLE
AWW!
HE'S GONNA HELP! AND HE SAID HE'D--
BING!
THERE! HE JUST SENT OVER HIS **CREDIT CARD.** I CAN BUY THE TICKETS ONLINE!
GREAT JOB, NEWT!
THERE'S A BUS IN A HALF HOUR...
BUT WE'RE GONNA NEED SOME **DISGUISES**.

THE BUS STATION IS JUST ACROSS THE STREET THERE.
BUS
DEPOT
EVERYONE READY?
CLARICE, THE FUR IS A DEAD GIVEAWAY.
fwippy
fwip
YOU WON'T NEED TO BE A **SEAL** ON THE **BUS**!!
YANK
CAN'T YOU PUT IT IN YOUR BAG??
HERE--WEAR THIS ON TOP! IT'LL LOOK LIKE A **FUR HOOD.**
VERY FASHIONABLE!
DINER
LET'S GO!

SNEAK SNEAK
BUS
DEPOT
GAS
BUS
DEPOT
DASH
THERE'S THE BUS! LET'S GO!
WAIT!
YOINK
tp tp tp
HOW ARE WE GONNA GET ON BOARD??
LOOK! IT'S THOSE **SQUATCH GUYS!**
tmp

HEY! YOU! WE'VE BEEN HEARING A LOT OF CHATTER ON YOUR RADIOS ABOUT "MISSING ASSETS!"
WHAT DID YOU LET OUT? WHAT ARE YOU HIDING?
FOLKS, WE'VE WARNED YOU BEFORE ABOUT TAPPING INTO OUR FREQUENCIES.
IF WE HAVE TO SEIZE YOUR RADIOS AGAIN WE WILL.
tp tp tp tp
THOSE RADIOS ARE PRIVATE PROPERTY! IF YOU DIDN'T WANT US TO LISTEN YOU'D USE STRONGER ENCRYPTION, WOULDN'T YOU??
DID YOU JUST ADMIT TO HACKING OUR FREQUENCIES?
NO! WHAT? MAYBE?! IT DOESN'T MATTER!
WHAT SORTS OF CREATURES GOT OUT??
WHAT ARE YOU HIDING IN THAT WEIRD FACILITY OUT THERE??
WE'RE NOT HIDING ANYTHING. WE'VE BEEN THROUGH THIS BEFORE--
WE HAVE SOLID EVIDENCE THAT YOU'RE KEEPING ALIENS...
AND CRYPTOZOOLOGICAL ENTITIES OUT THERE, AND IT SURE SOUNDS LIKE SOME OF THEM ESCAPED!
sssssip
YOU'RE CRAZY.
ARE YOU CALLING US CRAZY?!
YEP. GOT SOME ALIENS IN YOUR EARS? OR DID YOU JUST NOT HEAR ME?
MOVE ALONG, Y'ALL. I'M HEADING OUT AND I DON'T WANNA RUN YA OVER.
SHOO

VVVGGRRROOOOM!
RRMM
RRMM
WE KNOW YOU'RE HIDING **SOMETHING** AND WE'RE GONNA FIND OUT WHAT IT IS!
WE'RE THE FRATERNITY OF RESEARCHERS TO THE EXISTENCE OF ALL KNOWN INTELLIGENT SUPERNATURAL HUMANOIDS--
AND WE WILL **NOT STOP** UNTIL THE TRUTH IS **REVEALED**!!
STUART, STOP BEING SO DRAMATIC, DUDE!
WE'RE GONNA GET **ARRESTED** AGAIN!
THAT'S A MOUTHFUL.
SNERK-
I LIKE "THE SQUATCH GUYS" BETTER.
TWENTY-SIX HOURS TO D.C. Y'ALL GET SOME SHUT EYE. I'LL TURN OUT THE LIGHTS.
PHEW

zzZZ
zZzz
zZzz
Vrrrrrrrrrrrrrrrrr

CHAPTER FIVE

HIGHLY IRREGULAR

THEY EVEN HAVE A **BATHROOM** ON THIS THING!
DID YOU WASH YOUR HANDS?
...
...
-ROLL-
STOMP STOMP
DUCK
-SHRUG-
SO! TELL US ABOUT THIS POLITICIAN DAD OF YOURS.
UMMM...

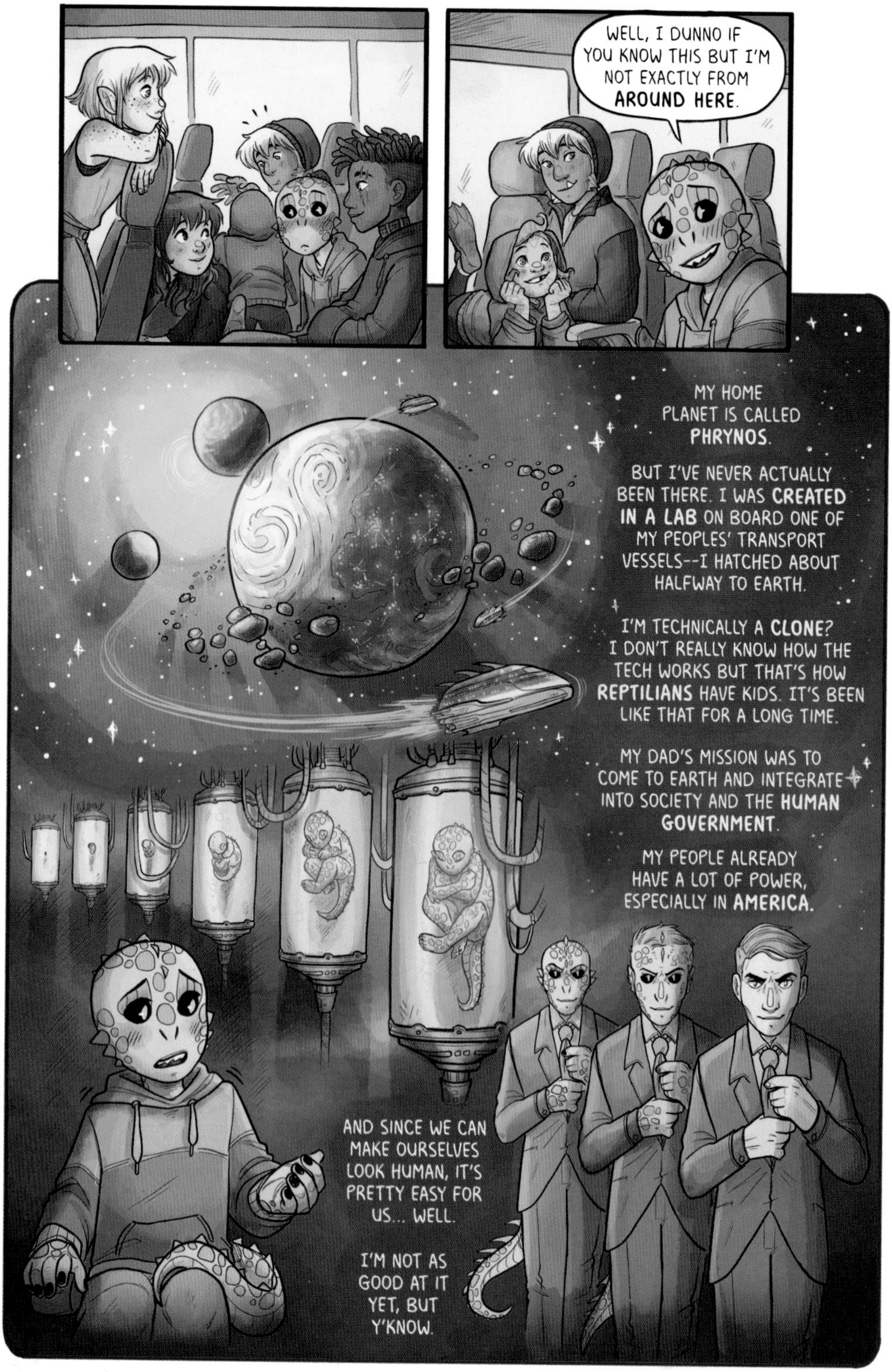
WELL, I DUNNO IF YOU KNOW THIS BUT I'M NOT EXACTLY FROM AROUND HERE.
MY HOME PLANET IS CALLED PHRYNOS.
BUT I'VE NEVER ACTUALLY BEEN THERE. I WAS CREATED IN A LAB ON BOARD ONE OF MY PEOPLES' TRANSPORT VESSELS--I HATCHED ABOUT HALFWAY TO EARTH.
I'M TECHNICALLY A CLONE? I DON'T REALLY KNOW HOW THE TECH WORKS BUT THAT'S HOW REPTILIANS HAVE KIDS. IT'S BEEN LIKE THAT FOR A LONG TIME.
MY DAD'S MISSION WAS TO COME TO EARTH AND INTEGRATE INTO SOCIETY AND THE HUMAN GOVERNMENT.
MY PEOPLE ALREADY HAVE A LOT OF POWER, ESPECIALLY IN AMERICA.
AND SINCE WE CAN MAKE OURSELVES LOOK HUMAN, IT'S PRETTY EASY FOR US... WELL.
I'M NOT AS GOOD AT IT YET, BUT Y'KNOW.

WHOA, WHOA, WHOA, WAIT A SECOND.
ARE YOU SAYING YOUR PEOPLE--ALIENS??--ARE TRYING TO TAKE OVER THE GOVERNMENT?!
WELL... YEAH?
WHAT THE HECK, NEWT?!
I NEVER WANTED ANYTHING TO DO WITH THAT! I LIKE HUMANS, AND I LIKE EARTH! IT'S MY DAD AND HIS PEOPLE THAT WANT TO CHANGE THINGS.
I NEVER FIT IN WITH THE OTHER REPTILIAN KIDS.
WE HAD TO LEARN ALL ABOUT EARTH, SO WE COULD COPY THE HUMANS AND ACT LIKE YOU.
BUT I DIDN'T WANT TO ACT. I WANTED TO JUST BE A HUMAN KID.
I TRIED TO MAKE FRIENDS WITH THE OTHERS BUT...
HEY! YOU WANNA PLAY?
WHY ARE YOU PRACTICING HUMAN MANNERISMS OUTSIDE OF LESSONS?
IT... LOOKED LIKE FUN?
FUN IS IRRELEVANT. YOU ARE STRANGE.

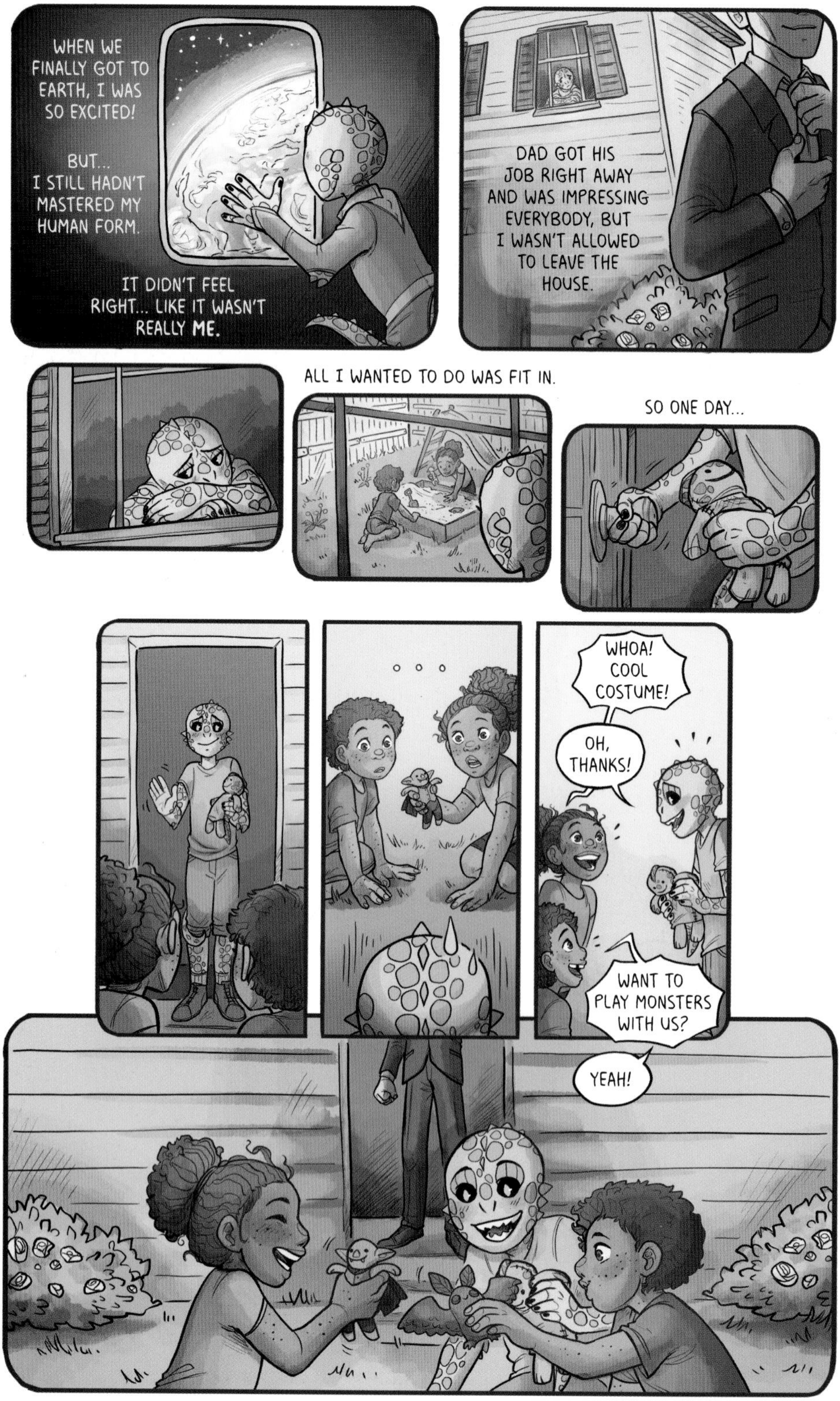
WHEN WE FINALLY GOT TO EARTH, I WAS SO EXCITED!
BUT... I STILL HADN'T MASTERED MY HUMAN FORM.
IT DIDN'T FEEL RIGHT... LIKE IT WASN'T REALLY ME.
DAD GOT HIS JOB RIGHT AWAY AND WAS IMPRESSING EVERYBODY, BUT I WASN'T ALLOWED TO LEAVE THE HOUSE.
ALL I WANTED TO DO WAS FIT IN.
SO ONE DAY...
WHOA! COOL COSTUME!
OH, THANKS!
WANT TO PLAY MONSTERS WITH US?
YEAH!

NEWTON!
UH, HI, DAD--
GET BACK INSIDE THIS INSTANT!
I GOT... I WAS REALLY IN TROUBLE. MY DAD SAID I HAD JEOPARDIZED THE MISSION.
AND I HAD TO GO AWAY UNTIL I COULD MASTER MY HUMAN FORM. SO HE SENT ME TO THE PLAYROOM.
YOUR DAD SOUNDS... INTENSE.
YEAH... BUT HE'S HELPING ME--U-US OUT NOW, ISN'T HE?
THAT HAS TO COUNT FOR SOMETHING, RIGHT?

WELL, MY DAD IS THE KING OF THE OCEAN!
WHAT?
Once upon a time
WAIT, IS THIS REAL OR ONE OF YOUR FAIRY TALES?
SHH!! DON'T INTERRUPT!
ONCE UPON A TIME...
...THERE WAS A LOVELY MAIDEN. THAT'S MY MOM!
THERE WAS ALSO A BIG AND SCARY KING (BUT ONLY ON THE OUTSIDE!). THAT'S MY DAD!
THEY MET BY THE SEASIDE AND FELL IN LOVE, SPENDING THEIR DREAMS TOGETHER EVERY NIGHT.

SOON, A LITTLE PRINCESS WAS BORN!
THAT'S ME!
BUT MY MOM HAD TO LEAVE ME WITH THE PLAYROOM BECAUSE SHE HAD TO **GO AWAY**...
PROBABLY TO DO SOMETHING **SUPER DANGEROUS** LIKE **FIGHT A DINOSAUR!**
BUT THAT'S OKAY, 'CUZ **OMAR** WAS THERE, AND NOW I GET TO PLAY WITH **YOU GUYS** EVERY DAY.
AND ONE DAY DADDY'S GONNA COME GET ME...
AND WE'LL **RULE THE WHOLE OCEAN!!**
THAT... SURE IS A DRAMATIC STORY, MAGGIE.
I KNOW!
TWO HOURS OUT FROM D.C., Y'ALL.

GREETINGS, NEWTON.
UH, HI?
NEWTON?
SHUT UP!
YOUR FATHER SENT US TO ESCORT YOU.
WHO ARE THEY?
OH, THEY'RE, UH... THE OTHER KIDS KEPT IN THE FACILITY. THEY'RE COMING TOO.
VERY WELL. WE HAVE A CAR WAITING. COME ALONG.

SLIiiiiDE
GRAB
WRONG POCKET, KID.
HEH... UH... MY BAD?
SCRAM.

THIS WAY. KEEP UP.
concierge
CONFERENCE ROOM 1
GREETINGS, NEWTON.
...HI, DAD.

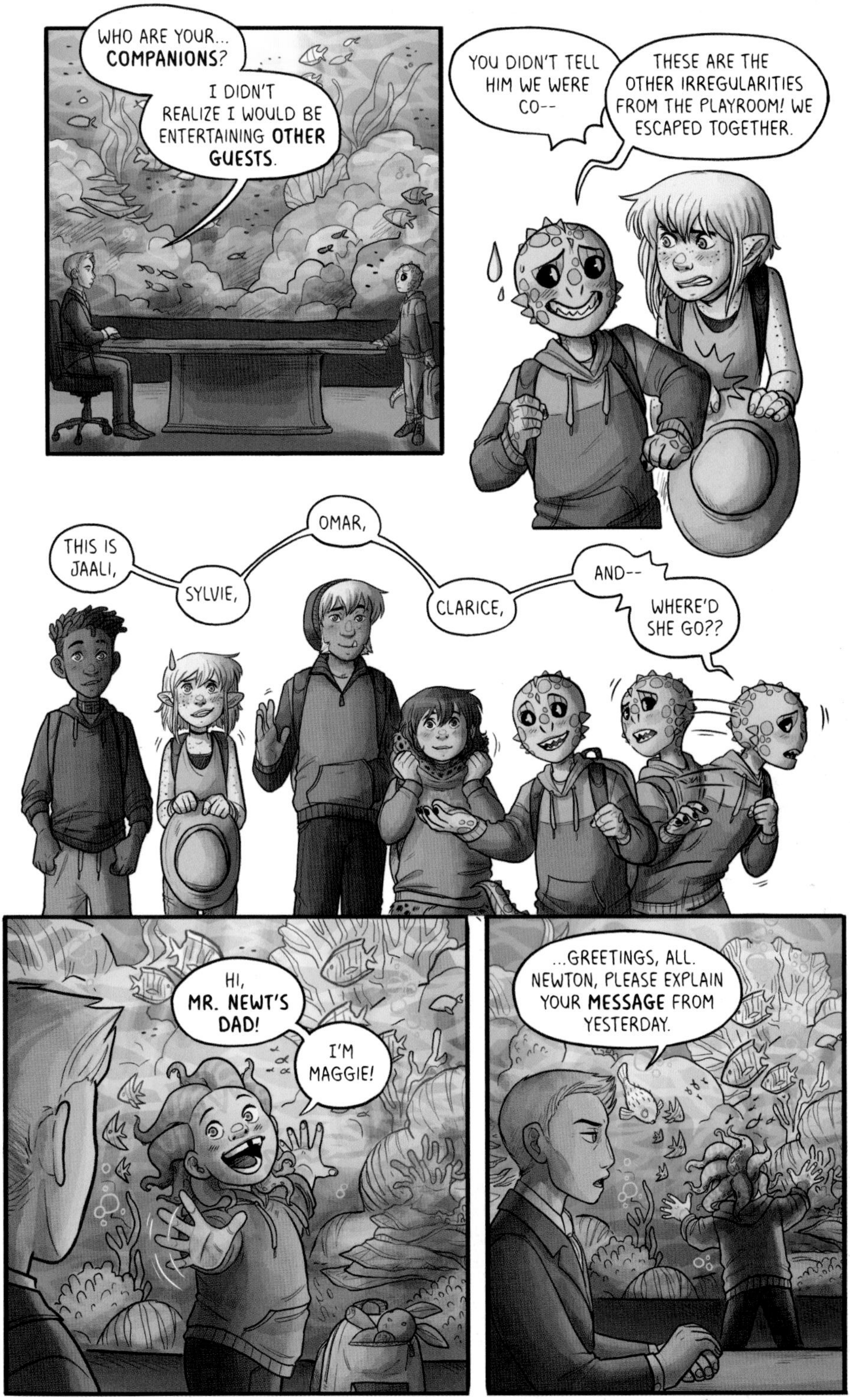

WHO ARE YOUR... COMPANIONS?
I DIDN'T REALIZE I WOULD BE ENTERTAINING OTHER GUESTS.
YOU DIDN'T TELL HIM WE WERE CO--
THESE ARE THE OTHER IRREGULARITIES FROM THE PLAYROOM! WE ESCAPED TOGETHER.
THIS IS JAALI,
SYLVIE,
OMAR,
CLARICE,
AND--
WHERE'D SHE GO??
HI, MR. NEWT'S DAD!
I'M MAGGIE!
...GREETINGS, ALL. NEWTON, PLEASE EXPLAIN YOUR MESSAGE FROM YESTERDAY.

THERE WAS A BREACH OF SECURITY AT THE PLAYROOM. ONE OF THE AGENTS DOUBLE-CROSSED THEM.
WE STARTED GETTING **THREATENING MESSAGES** AND **BREAK-INS** TO OUR ROOMS, SO THE OTHER AGENTS THOUGHT THEY SHOULD MOVE US FOR SAFETY.
BUT THE DOUBLE-AGENT, **AGENT CLARK,** ENDED UP DRIVING OUR TRANSPORT...
THERE WAS AN INCIDENT AND ANOTHER AGENT WAS... KILLED. **SYLVIE** SAVED US ALL BY FORCING AGENT CLARK TO CRASH THE CAR, AND WE WALKED THROUGH THE DESERT TO FIND A BUS TO...
TO BRING US TO **YOU.**
WAS AGENT CLARK WORKING ALONE?
I'M NOT SURE...
IN THE CAR, HE SAID HE HAD TO TAKE US OR **HE** WOULD KILL HIM.
WE DON'T KNOW WHO "HE" IS.
WERE YOU FOLLOWED?
I DON'T THINK SO. THE BUS WAS **EMPTY** THE WHOLE RIDE HERE.

OH, HI, CLARICE! ARE YOU HERE TO TALK TO THE FISH TOO?
THEY **REALLY** LIKE ME!
LOOK!
CLAP CLAP
WHAT'S YOUR **NAME**? WHAT DO THEY FEED YOU HERE? IS IT **NICE** IN THE TANK? ARE YOU FRIENDS WITH THE **OTHER** FISH? ARE THEY NICE TOO?
BLUP
DID YOU HEAR THAT?? HE SAYS THEY EAT **FISH FLAKES**! WHAT THE HECK IS A **FISH FLAKE**??
HA HA HA HA HA HA HA

IT SOUNDS LIKE YOU HAVE BEEN THROUGH QUITE THE ORDEAL.
TYPICAL **HUMANS**.
MISHANDLING **DELICATE MATTERS** SEEMS TO BE ONE OF THEIR **SPECIALITIES**.
PUSH
I JUST KNEW SOMETHING LIKE THIS WOULD HAPPEN.
THOSE **FOOLS** RUNNING THE PLAYROOM NEVER HAD PROPER SECURITY TO BEGIN WITH.
HOW COULD THEY HANDLE SUCH A COMPLICATED ISSUE?
NO MATTER. I KEPT UP **MY END** OF THE **BARGAIN.**
TP TP TP
IT IS NO FAULT OF MINE IF THEY COULD NOT KEEP THEIRS.
B...BARGAIN?

NEWTON, YOU GAVE ME NO CHOICE. YOUR **INEPTITUDE** EXPOSED ME.
I DON'T UNDERSTAND...
THE GOVERNMENT WAS SUSPICIOUS OF ME FOR A LONG TIME, AND WERE LOOKING FOR ANY EVIDENCE THEY COULD GET.
YOUR **LITTLE STUNT** WAS JUST WHAT THEY HAD BEEN WAITING FOR. ONE OF THEIR PEOPLE TOOK THAT PHOTO THROUGH THE FENCE.
SO I HAD TO MAKE A **DEAL**, NEWTON.
THEY PROMISED NOT TO EXPOSE ME AND TO LET ME KEEP MY POSITION...
IF THEY COULD TAKE **CUSTODY** OF **YOU**.
FOR STUDY, I ASSUMED.
YOU... YOU **GAVE ME UP**??
IT WASN'T A DIFFICULT DECISION TO MAKE. I HAD TO PROTECT EVERYTHING I'D BUILT. PROTECT THE SECURITY OF THE MISSION.
OUR MISSION.

YOU CHOSE TO PROTECT THE MISSION OVER **ME**? I'M YOUR **SON**!!
THE MISSION IS THE **ULTIMATE** PRIORITY, YOU SHOULD KNOW THAT.
YOU ARE **NOT** HUMAN, NO MATTER HOW MUCH YOU **WISH** TO BE ONE!
I NEVER HAD A **CHOICE** IN THIS!
THIS BEHAVIOR IS **HIGHLY IRREGULAR.** EMOTIONS LIKE THIS ARE NOT REQUIRED. I'M BEGINNING TO SUSPECT THERE WAS A **DEFECT** IN YOUR CLONING POD.
I'M NOT A DEFECT!
OBVIOUSLY **SOMETHING** IS WRONG WITH YOU.
YOU HAVE FORMED **ATTACHMENTS** TO THIS GROUP.
THIS IS YOUR **FINAL CHANCE**, NEWTON. COME WITH ME.
COME HOME.
sniff
snrk
WE WILL TRAVEL TO PHRYNOS TO CORRECT YOUR... **ISSUES.** YOU WILL FINALLY BE A PROPER REPTILIAN.
YOU WILL FINALLY MAKE ME **PROUD.**

tremble
plip
...NO.
WHAT DID YOU SAY TO ME?!
I SAID NO!
I WANT NOTHING TO DO WITH YOU OR... OR THE STUPID MISSION! THESE ARE MY FRIENDS! THE PLAYROOM WAS MORE HOME THAN IT EVER WAS WITH YOU!
WE'RE STAYING TOGETHER, AND YOU CAN'T CHANGE ME!
MATH
FINE.
SINCE YOUR MIND IS MADE UP.
YOU WILL HAVE NO FURTHER CONTACT WITH ME.
BEST OF LUCK.

snatch
TIME TO GO, MAGGIE.
OKAY.
fwip
BYE!
STOMP STOMP
...NEWT?
I'M SO SORRY.
I'M SO SORRY I DRAGGED YOU INTO THIS--AND NOW WE HAVE **NOWHERE TO GO!**
IT'S OKAY, WE'LL FIGURE SOMETHING OUT.

ARE YOU OKAY?
I'M... I DON'T KNOW.
I HADN'T SEEN HIM IN SO LONG... I HOPED HE'D BE DIFFERENT. BUT HE HASN'T CHANGED AT ALL.
...AND APPARENTLY I'VE CHANGED TOO MUCH.
WHAT HE SAID BACK THERE, ABOUT YOU BEING DEFECTIVE? YOU KNOW NONE OF US...
THINK THAT ABOUT YOU, RIGHT? THAT WAS COLD AND MEAN AND CRUEL.
WELL, OF COURSE IT WAS COLD, HE'S COLD-BLOODED!
HE'S A REPTILE!
HA HA HA HA HA HA HA HA HA HA HA HA
HA... HA... HEH... sniff...
SOB

CHAPTER SIX

TWO HOUSES

SO WHAT ARE WE GONNA DO?
I'M NOT SURE...
VVRRRRRRRRRRRRRR
NO WAY.
IS THAT--
IT IS!
IT'S THE SQUATCH GUYS!
F.R.E.A.KISH
VVVRRRRRRRRRRRRRR
QUICK! THIS WAY!

tmp
YOU'RE NOT GETTING AWAY THIS TIME, KID!
WHERE'D THEY GO?!
CAN'T HAVE GONE FAR--KEEP LOOKING!
HEH!
OOF!
HEY! WATCH WHERE YOU'RE GO--
shhhh!

VRRRRRRRRRRRMM
HOW DID THEY FOLLOW US ALL THE WAY HERE??
I HAVE NO IDEA!
WHO ARE YOU?
I COULD ASK YOU THE SAME THING!
BRUSH BRUSH
WAIT A SECOND--
YOU'RE THE KID WITH THE BODYGUARDS!
THEY WEREN'T MY BODYGUARDS!
WELL, I DIDN'T TAKE THE STUPID WALLET, ALL RIGHT?
YOU GONNA TURN INTO SOME KIND OF LIZARD DUDE TOO??
!

YO!
OKAY, THAT'S PRETTY COOL, ACTUALLY. MY BAD.
WELL, IT'S A PLEASURE MEETING YOU ALL. GOOD TO KNOW WE'RE NOT THE ONLY **MONSTERS** AROUND.
"WE?"
AAOOOOOOOO
THERE!
DOWN THERE! YOU CAN'T RUN, SNEAK THIEF!
CRAP...
UNFORTUNATELY, I DON'T HAVE TIME FOR PLEASANTRIES--
I AM CURRENTLY BEING **CHASED,**
AND I ABSOLUTELY MUST KEEP MOVING.
YOU SHOULD TOO--YOU DON'T WANT TO GET CAUGHT BY THE DUDES THAT ARE CHASING ME.
I'M OFF TO THE **HIDEOUT!**
SPIN
SHWOOP!
POP
YOU COMING OR WHAT?

WHO'S CHASING YOU??
fwip!
fwip!
WHO'S CHASING YOU?!
fwip!
THEY WENT THIS WAY!
OVER HERE!
GAH!
HERE-- GET IN!
shffff
COME OUT, KITTY CAT!
YOU CAN'T HIDE FOREVER!
WHERE'D THEY GO?!
THAT VAN WITH ALL THE STICKERS HAS BEEN CHASING US FOR DAYS BECAUSE WE'RE IRREGULARITIES.
YOU?
I MAAAAY HAVE LIBERATED SOME OF THESE DUDES' WALLETS?
-SNORT- HA HEE HA HEE HA HA HA

COAST IS CLEAR-- C'MON!
WAIT A MINUTE! YOU STILL HAVEN'T TOLD US WHO YOU ARE!
I'M **TIBBS**!
CLOSED
CLOS D
WELCOME, FRIENDS--
BOW
TO THE LAIR OF THE **MALKINS**!

HOME SWEET HOME!
WHO YOU GOT THERE, TIBBS?
PICKED UP A COUPLE OF STRAYS ON MY WAY BACK!

YOU JUST BROUGHT THEM HERE? TIBBS, YOU KNOW--
I KNOW I'M NOT SUPPOSED TO SHOW **OUTSIDERS**.
BUT LOOK! THEY'RE IRREGULARITIES LIKE **US**!
HI!
PULL
ARE YOU SURE THEY'RE NOT WORKING FOR THE **JACKALS**?
THE WHO?
SEE! THEY'RE NEW IN TOWN! JUST ARRIVED THIS MORNING.
THEY WERE BEING CHASED-- I THOUGHT MAYBE **THE BOSS** COULD HELP THEM.
...FINE.
COME ON THIS WAY!
ARE YOU SURE ABOUT THIS?
I HONESTLY HAVE NO IDEA.
COME IN, CHILDREN.

TIBBS, DEAR, INTRODUCE ME TO YOUR FRIENDS.
IS THAT A TALKING CAT?!
AH, YES, MY APOLOGIES.
IS THIS MORE COMFORTABLE FOR YOU?

IT'S... A BIT BETTER, YES.
EVERYONE, THIS IS **CAT SITH.**
THE CAT SITH??
LIKE FROM THE **FAIRY TALES**??
THE VERY SAME. DON'T BE ALARMED, IT'S NOT OFTEN I'M HOST TO A **WISP.**
BUT REST ASSURED, YOU ARE SAFE HERE AS MY GUESTS.
SO... WHAT BRINGS YOU TO OUR HUMBLE ABODE?
WE'VE... BEEN TRAVELING FOR A WHILE. WE JUST ARRIVED IN D.C. TODAY.
OUR ORIGINAL PLAN... DIDN'T WORK OUT, AND WE HAVE NO PLACE TO STAY. TIBBS FOUND US BY ACCIDENT--
THOSE **F.R.E.A.K.I.S.H. GUYS** HAD US PINNED IN AN ALLEYWAY.
OH, **THOSE** IDIOTS. I DIDN'T REALIZE THEY WERE BACK IN TOWN.
YOU KNOW OF THEM?
SURE DO.
flop

THEY'RE A GROUP OF CONSPIRACY THEORISTS WHO'VE GOTTEN A BIT TOO CLOSE FOR COMFORT TO OUR VARIOUS COMMUNITIES. WE'VE LED THEM ON MORE WILD-GOOSE CHASES THAN I WANT TO REMEMBER. THEY'RE NOT DANGEROUS, JUST UTTERLY ANNOYING.
LAST I HEARD THEY WERE HEADED FOR NEVADA. SOMETHING ABOUT ALIENS AND AREA 51.
COUGH
glance
DON'T WORRY, YOU'RE SAFE FROM THEM HERE.
YOU'RE WELCOME TO STAY THE NIGHT, BUT IN RETURN I HAVE A FAVOR TO ASK.
AS I'M SURE YOU'VE GATHERED, THESE ARE THE MALKINS.
BUT WE'RE NOT ALONE IN THIS CITY. UNFORTUNATELY, WE OFTEN CLASH WITH A GROUP THAT CALLS THEMSELVES THE JACKALS.
AS PETTY AS OUR SQUABBLES HAVE BEEN, THE JACKALS RECENTLY CROSSED THE LINE.
THEY ACCUSED US OF CAPTURING ONE OF THEIR MEMBERS.

AND AS **REVENGE**, THEY'VE TAKEN ONE OF OURS. **JAYLA**.
BUT YOU **DIDN'T** KIDNAP THEIR FRIEND?
OF COURSE NOT!
WHAT REASON WOULD WE HAVE?
BESIDES, OUR METHODS ARE MUCH **QUIETER** AND **MORE SUBTLE**.
IN RETURN FOR ROOM AND BOARD HERE, I WOULD ASK THAT YOU RESCUE OUR MISSING MALKIN.
TOSS
CATCH
THE JACKALS KNOW TO WATCH OUT FOR US, BUT THEY WILL NEVER SEE YOU COMING.
TIBBS CAN GIVE YOU MORE INFORMATION AND LEAD YOU TO THE JACKAL HIDEOUT TOMORROW.
THEY KNOW THIS CITY LIKE THE BACK OF THEIR HAND.
FOR TONIGHT, EAT, SLEEP, REST.
THANK YOU, SIR.
THANKS, MR. KITTY!
YOU'RE WELCOME, MY DEAR.
THANKS!
ISN'T THIS **AMAZING**?? ALL THESE IRREGULARITIES LIVING RIGHT UNDER THE CITY'S NOSE!
IT IS IMPRESSIVE.
munch munch

ARE WE GONNA LIVE HERE NOW?
I DON'T KNOW... WE HAVE TO TRY TO RESCUE THEIR FRIEND, AND IT COULD BE DANGEROUS.
bomp!
AHHH, IT'LL BE FINE-- YOU'RE WITH **ME**! THEY'RE A BUNCH OF **PUSHOVERS** ANYWAY.
DIDN'T THEY CHASE YOU ALL OVER THE CITY TODAY?
AHEM. WELL.
IT'LL BE FINE. JUST GOTTA BE SNEAKY, Y'KNOW? GET IN, GRAB JAYLA, GET OUT.
wiggle
WORKS FOR ME! I COULD GET USED TO LIVING WITHOUT A SCHEDULE.
WITHOUT GETTING CHASED THROUGH THE DESERT.
WAIT WAIT--YOU WERE CHASED THROUGH THE **DESERT**??
OH MAN! YOU DON'T KNOW THE HALF OF IT!
HA HA HA
HA

snooore
snerk
ZZZ
tp tp
tp
ZZZ
swing swing
HEY.
OH, HEY, LIZARD DUDE! CAN'T SLEEP?
NAH, NOT THAT TIRED. HAD A CRAZY DAY.
WANT TO TALK ABOUT IT?
ACTUALLY, I WANTED TO ASK YOU ABOUT SOMETHING ELSE.
WHAT'S ON YOUR MIND?
UMM... I HOPE THIS ISN'T RUDE OR ANYTHING? BUT MR. SITH CALLED YOU "THEY" EARLIER? WHAT DOES THAT MEAN?
THAT'S MY PRONOUN.
YOUR WHAT?
LIKE, JAALI AND OMAR ARE "HE," SYLVIE AND MAGGIE AND CLARICE ARE "SHE."
I'M "THEY!"
SO, LIKE... "HE" IS FOR BOYS AND "SHE" IS FOR GIRLS...
"THEY" IS FOR... YOU?

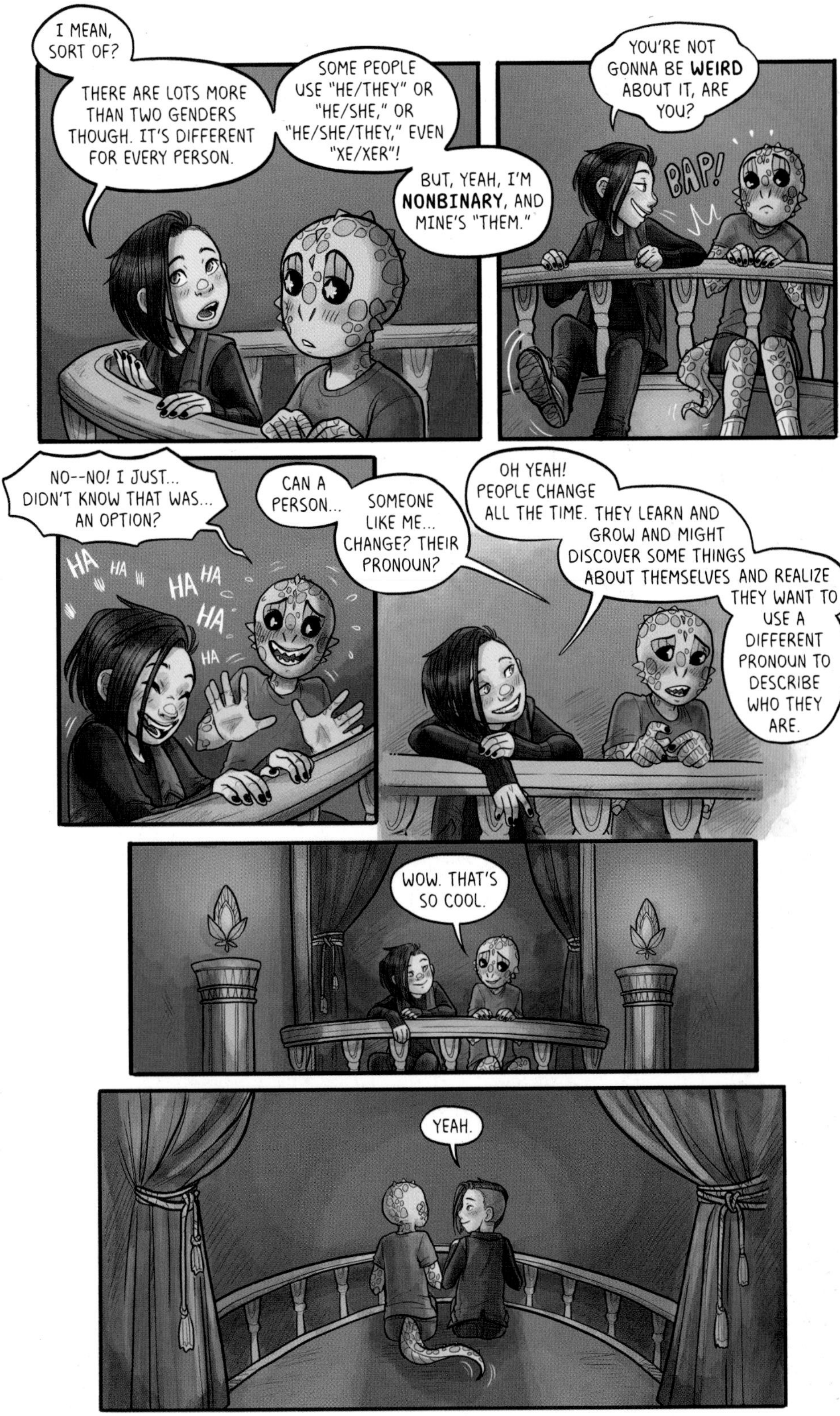
I MEAN, SORT OF?
THERE ARE LOTS MORE THAN TWO GENDERS THOUGH. IT'S DIFFERENT FOR EVERY PERSON.
SOME PEOPLE USE "HE/THEY" OR "HE/SHE," OR "HE/SHE/THEY," EVEN "XE/XER"!
BUT, YEAH, I'M **NONBINARY**, AND MINE'S "THEM."
YOU'RE NOT GONNA BE **WEIRD** ABOUT IT, ARE YOU?
BAP!
NO--NO! I JUST... DIDN'T KNOW THAT WAS... AN OPTION?
HA HA HA HA HA HA HA
CAN A PERSON...
SOMEONE LIKE ME... CHANGE? THEIR PRONOUN?
OH YEAH! PEOPLE CHANGE ALL THE TIME. THEY LEARN AND GROW AND MIGHT DISCOVER SOME THINGS ABOUT THEMSELVES AND REALIZE THEY WANT TO USE A DIFFERENT PRONOUN TO DESCRIBE WHO THEY ARE.
WOW. THAT'S SO COOL.
YEAH.

ALL RIGHT, SO! THE MISSING MALKIN'S NAME IS **JAYLA**.
WE THINK THE JACKALS TOOK HER ABOUT A WEEK AGO.
YOU **THINK**?
WELL, WE SAW THOSE DOGS SKULKING AROUND OUR HIDEOUT AND COULDN'T FIND JAYLA ANYWHERE. WHO ELSE COULD IT BE?
HMM...
ANYWAY, I'M GONNA LEAD YOU TO THEIR HIDEOUT. I KNOW YOU'RE NEW TO THE **SNEAK-THIEF LIFE**, SO YOU HAVE TO FOLLOW ALL MY ORDERS AND DO **EXACTLY** WHAT I SAY.
YOU'RE THE LEADER? WHO PUT YOU IN CHARGE??
CAT SITH! AND I'M THE BEST AT STEALING AND SNEAKING AND STUFF!
OH, REALLY? THEN WHERE'S YOUR **WALLET**?
PAT
PAT
PAT
PAT
PFFFF!
FINE, YOU GOT ME THAT TIME. BUT SERIOUSLY, FOLLOW MY LEAD.
HEE HEE!

THERE IT IS. WE'VE GOTTA BE CAREFUL NOW, AND NOT LET THEM CATCH US.
THESE DOGS LIKE TO BITE.
WHAT?
I MEAN, THEY'RE CALLED THE JACKALS FOR A REASON. THEY CAN TURN INTO WOLVES.
THIS IS A GANG OF WERE-WOLVES?!
flap flap
YEAH, WELL, YOU'RE A WEREBEAR, AREN'T YOU? WE'LL BE FINE!
HOW DO WE GET IN?
I... DIDN'T THINK THAT FAR AHEAD.
OH, PERFECT.
LOOK AT THE LADDER THINGIES!
OH YEAH, THE FIRE ESCAPE! GOOD IDEA, MAGS!
tp tp tp tp
HOP HOP
rattle

DO YOU SEE JAYLA?
NOT YET. KEEP LOOKING!
THAT'S THEIR LEADER, DINAH.
snag
PULL
TUG TUG
YANK
QUIET!
CLATTER

WHAT WAS THAT??
IS SOMEONE OUTSIDE?
GO LOOK!
UM, MISS DINAH? HARRIS SAID HE NEEDS YOUR HELP DOWNSTAIRS?
HMPH. ALL RIGHT. I'LL HEAD DOWN.
PHEW!
OKAY, GOTTA KEEP LOOKIN--
ACK!
WHAT ARE YOU DOING?
SHE'S ONE OF THE JACKALS!
GET READY FOR A FIGHT!

hissssss
WHOA, WHOA, WHOA! I JUST WANNA TALK!
YOU CAN'T TRUST A JACKAL!
I JUST SAVED YOUR BUTTS FROM GETTING SPOTTED! I TOLD DINAH TO GO DOWNSTAIRS.
YOU'RE HERE LOOKING FOR THE MISSING MALKIN, AREN'T YOU? **WE DON'T HAVE HER**. AND WE'RE STILL MISSING ONE OF **OURS** TOO--
MY BROTHER RAY. I'M TRYING TO FIND HIM, BUT THE REST OF THE JACKALS
ARE TOO CAUGHT UP IN FIGHTING THE MALKINS TO **HELP ME.**
SOUNDS LIKE SHE'S TELLING THE TRUTH, TIBBS.
FINE. LET'S TALK. BUT THE FIRST SIGN OF A TRAP, WE'RE BUSTING OUR WAY OUTTA HERE!
FINE BY ME, **SCAREDY-CAT.**
AM NOT!
SHHH!

I'M **ADDIE.** MY BROTHER WENT MISSING ABOUT A WEEK AGO.
THAT'S WHEN JAYLA WENT MISSING TOO, RIGHT?
YEAH.
I DON'T THINK THE MALKINS TOOK RAY--HE WAS ACTING **WEIRD** IN THE DAYS BEFORE HE DISAPPEARED.
HE WAS DISTANT, WOULDN'T TALK TO ANYONE.
NOT EVEN ME.
ALL THE REST OF THE JACKALS THOUGHT YOU MALKINS TOOK HIM--
WE **DIDN'T!**
I KNOW, I KNOW! BUT EVERYONE **THINKS** IT!
AND ALL THE MALKINS THINK WE TOOK ONE OF YOURS FOR REVENGE! IT'S ALL TWISTED UP, AND WE HAVE TO FIX IT.
AND I WANT TO KNOW WHERE MY BROTHER IS.
CAN'T YOU JUST **WOLF IT UP** AND FOLLOW HIS SCENT TRAIL?
OH NO, I'M NOT A WOLF.
YOU'RE **NOT??**
NO, BUT **MY BROTHER IS.** HE JOINED THE JACKALS WHEN WE WERE YOUNGER, AND THEY TOOK US BOTH IN.
EVEN THOUGH I'M JUST A **HUMAN.**
THEY'RE REALLY NOT AS BAD AS YOU MALKINS SEEM TO THINK.
THE WOLVES FOLLOWED HIS SCENT AS FAR AS THEY COULD, BUT IT ENDS RIGHT NEAR THE **MALKIN HIDEOUT.** THAT'S WHY THEY THINK YOU'VE GOT RAY.

BUT IT SEEMED OFF TO ME... I SEARCHED ON MY OWN AND THE ONLY THING I FOUND WAS HIS PHONE.
10:02
BUT IT'S LOCKED--I CAN'T GET IT OPEN. I'M STUCK.
10:02
NO PROBLEM. NEWT?
I'M ON IT!
CRACK
SO HOW LONG DOES THIS NORMALLY TA--
tappa tap
tap tap
DONE!
HOLY CRAP, THAT WAS FAST! I'VE BEEN TRYING FOR A WEEK!
YOU'RE THE BEST!
CAN YOU FIND HIS LAST LOCATION? OR, LIKE, TEXTS OR CALLS OR SOMETHING?
YEAH, LET ME JUST...
WAIT.
HEY, TIBBS? WHAT DOES JAYLA LOOK LIKE?
UH, BLACK HAIR IN BRAIDS, YELLOW EYES LIKE MINE, KINDA SHORT?
WITH PINK STREAKS IN HER HAIR?
YEAH! WHAT? HOW??
LOOK.

W-
WHAT??
HE NEVER TOLD ME ABOUT--
THEY WERE **TOGETHER**??
YEAH.
DO THE TEXTS SAY WHERE THEY WENT?
THEY KEEP TALKING ABOUT "**THE SANCTUARY**"?
IT COMES UP A BUNCH OF TIMES. AND... HERE! THEY PLANNED TO RUN AWAY!
THEY LEFT A WEEK AGO. HE MUST HAVE FORGOTTEN HIS PHONE.
WHAT'S THE SANCTUARY?
IT SOUNDS LIKE IT'S A SAFE HAVEN FOR IRREGULARITIES... OUT WEST IN WASHINGTON STATE.
HE JUST LEFT?! WITHOUT SAYING GOODBYE?! **QUÉ IMBÉCIL**!
WHUMP
SO BOTH SIDES THINK THEIR MEMBER WAS KIDNAPPED, BUT THEY LEFT TOGETHER WITHOUT TELLING ANYONE.
THEY WERE SO AFRAID OF THE GANGS TRYING TO **BREAK THEM UP**.
THIS IS **SO** MESSED UP.
THEY NEED TO TALK THIS OUT SO THE FIGHTING CAN STOP--
BUT HOW DO WE GET THEM IN THE SAME PLACE? WILL THEY **TRUST** EACH OTHER?
NO. THE MALKINS WILL THINK THE JACKALS ARE SETTING UP A TRAP.
THE JACKALS WILL THINK THE SAME THING. THE ONLY WAY TO GET THEM TOGETHER WOULD BE TO **TRICK THEM** INTO IT.
...
...
I HAVE AN ABSOLUTELY HORRIBLE, WONDERFUL, **TERRIBLE** IDEA...

HELP!
THE MALKINS ARE KIDNAPPING ME NOW TOO!
AFTER THEM, HURRY!
THEY WON'T GET AWAY WITH IT THIS TIME!

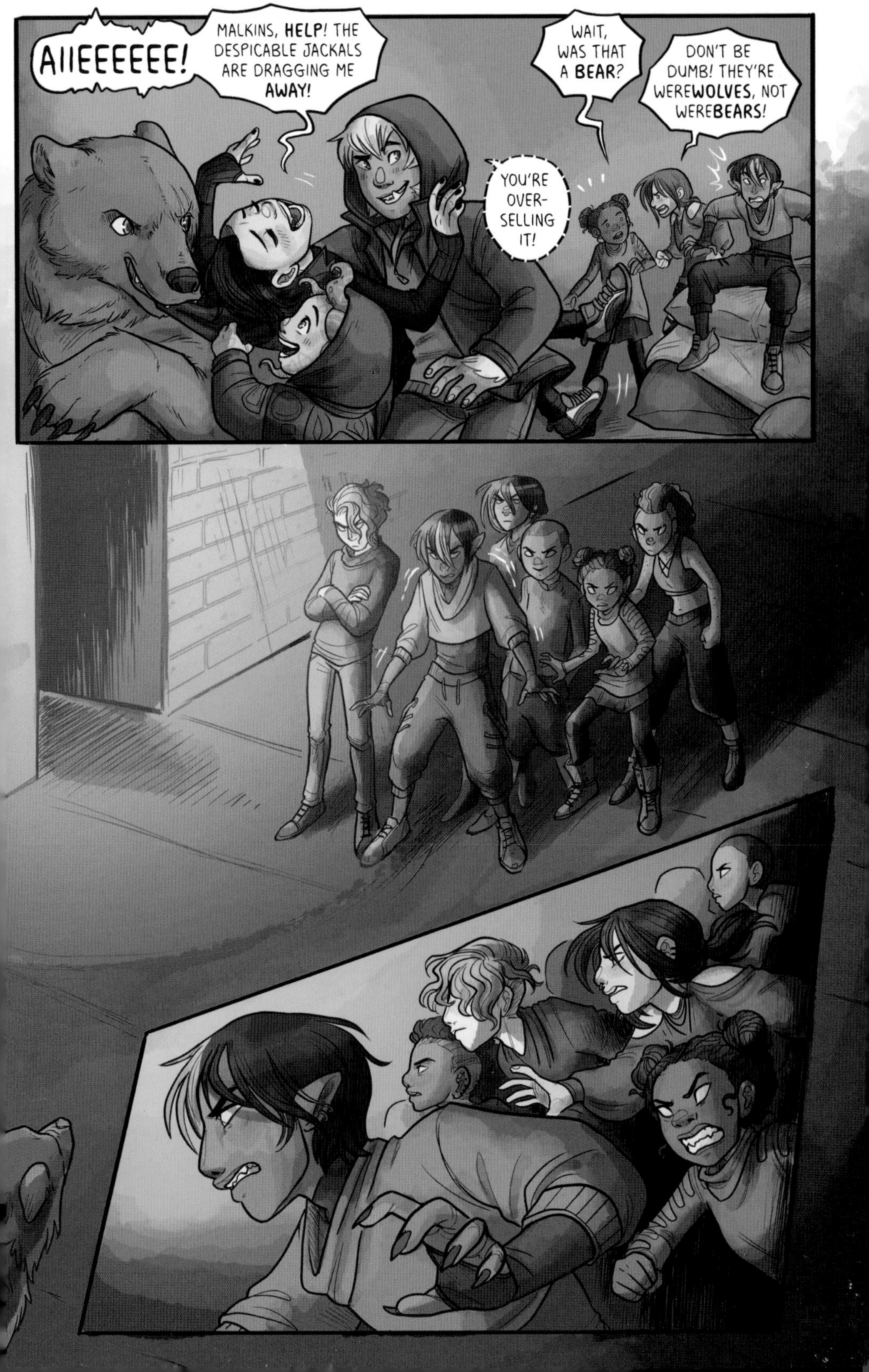
AIIEEEEEE!
MALKINS, HELP! THE DESPICABLE JACKALS ARE DRAGGING ME AWAY!
YOU'RE OVER-SELLING IT!
WAIT, WAS THAT A BEAR?
DON'T BE DUMB! THEY'RE WEREWOLVES, NOT WEREBEARS!

YOU! GIVE ADDIE BACK! SHE'S DONE NOTHING TO YOU!
CEASE YOUR BARKING, DOG. WE DON'T HAVE ADDIE. RETURN TIBBS TO US.
TIBBS? THAT STREETCAT? WE DON'T HAVE THEM!
HIIISS
SSS
LIAR.
SNEAK!
BRUTE.
COWARD!
SSSNAAARL
SHWOOP!
WE'RE HERE!
WAIT!
SORRY WE HAD TO TRICK YOU--
ADDIE, WHAT IS THE MEANING OF THIS?!
TIBBS, WHAT HAVE YOU DONE?
WE HAD TO!
YOU WON'T STOP FIGHTING LONG ENOUGH TO HEAR THE TRUTH!
WE KNOW WHAT HAPPENED TO RAY AND JAYLA!

HUFF
HUFF
SPEAK THEN.
THIS IS RAY'S.
NEWT WAS ABLE TO UNLOCK IT AND CHECK THROUGH HIS PHOTOS AND MESSAGES.
HE AND JAYLA WERE **TOGETHER**.
WHAT?!
THEY FELL IN LOVE! LOOK AT THEM-- LOOK AT HOW **HAPPY** THEY ARE!
SO THEY RAN AWAY TOGETHER.
BUT YOU FOUGHT SO MUCH AND WERE SO DIVIDED, THEY KNEW THAT YOU WOULD TRY TO END THEIR RELATIONSHIP.
YOU **DROVE THEM AWAY**.

WHAT HAVE WE DONE?
I'M SO SORRY, BABY. WE GOT SO CARRIED AWAY...
WE NEVER MEANT TO DRIVE AWAY OUR FAMILY.
WE WERE WRONG IN THIS INSTANCE.
BUT I STILL DO NOT TRUST YOU OR YOUR DOGS.
SAME TO YOU, CAT!
YOU'RE DOING IT AGAIN!!
YOU HAVE TO TALK TO EACH OTHER!
YOU WERE WRONG THIS TIME, WHO'S TO SAY YOU HAVEN'T BEEN WRONG BEFORE?!
. . .

...VERY WELL. FOR THE GOOD OF BOTH OUR HOUSES, WE SHOULD WORK TOWARD **EASING THE TENSION.**
I'LL **PLAY NICE** IF YOU DO, SITH.
I LOOK FORWARD TO... FUTURE... COOPERATION.
...
...DITTO.

WE DID IT!!
I CAN'T BELIEVE THAT **WORKED**!
ARE YOU TWO GONNA BE OKAY HANDLING THIS ALLIANCE?
SEEMS LIKE IT'LL BE TOUGH...
OF **COURSE** WE WILL!
WE'LL KEEP THEM ON THEIR TOES--
MAKE SURE THEY DON'T **KILL** EACH OTHER.
WHAT ARE YOU GOING TO DO NOW?
SITH SAID YOU CAN STAY A WHILE, IF YOU WANT TO.

WE CAN'T REALLY STICK AROUND... NOT WITH **F.R.E.A.K.I.S.H.** ON OUR HEELS.
WE WOULDN'T WANT TO RISK EXPOSING THE JACKALS OR MALKINS.
MAYBE YOU CAN FOLLOW BEHIND RAY AND JAYLA? FIND THAT **SANCTUARY** THEY WERE TALKING ABOUT?
THAT'S WHAT WE WERE THINKING TOO.
HERE, TAKE RAY'S PHONE.
ONCE YOU GET THERE, TELL HIM TO CALL ME, FOR HEAVEN'S SAKE.
-SNIFF-
THANK YOU ALL SO MUCH!
I'M GLAD I TRIED TO PICKPOCKET YOUR BODYGUARD.
I **TOLD** YOU! HE WASN'T MY BODYGUARD--

SIR...
SIR, I...
YOU LOST THEM.
BUT I'M ON THEIR TRAIL! I HAVE ASSETS FOLLOWING THEM--THEY'RE IN D.C.! I'LL GET THEM BACK I SWEAR--
tremble

YOU'VE FAILED ME, AND YOU KNOW THE **CONSEQUENCES**.
sSShhhffff
NO! NO, **WAIT**-- I KNOW WHERE THEY ARE!
YOU NEED ME!
sSShhfff
A CLEVER GAMBIT, BUT YOU'VE ALREADY **LOST**, CLARK. I KNOW WHERE THEY ARE, AND THEY'LL FIND THEIR WAY
TO ME WITHOUT YOUR ASSISTANCE. MY TRAP IS SET. ALL I NEED NOW IS **PATIENCE**.
SLAM
NO! **NO, PLEASE!**
sSShhff
sSSh
NO! NO! AAAAAGH!

SNAP
WAVE
...SIR?

DISPOSE OF OUR **GUEST,** MY DEAR.
HE HAS OVERSTAYED HIS WELCOME.
GASP!
OH, AND GET ME IN CONTACT WITH CLARK'S "ASSETS" IN THE CAPITAL.
I BELIEVE IT'S THOSE **F.R.E.A.K.I.S.H.** IMBECILES?
SHUDDER
Y-YES, SIR.
I WANT UPDATES ON THE LOCATION OF MY **PREY.**
YES, SIR.
I WANT TO BE INFORMED OF EACH AND EVERY MOVE...
THIS HUNT IS ONLY JUST BEGINNING.

CHAPTER SEVEN

CROSS COUNTRY

-chatter-
-chatter-
-mumble-
-chatter-
SO I KNOW IT'S IN WASHINGTON STATE-- THAT'S WHERE RAY AND JAYLA WERE HEADED.
THEY HAVE A COUPLE OF MESSAGES BACK AND FORTH ABOUT BUS TICKETS AND STUFF...
BUT NO ADDRESSES.
CAN'T YOU JUST... LIKE... GOOGLE IT?
OH SURE, JUST SEARCH "HI, WHERE CAN A GROUP OF SIX MONSTERS THAT MAY OR MAY NOT INCLUDE...
A BEAR, A SELKIE, A YETI, AN ALIEN, A WILL-O-THE-WISP, AND WHATEVER MAGGIE IS, GO HIDE BECAUSE THE GOVERNMENT IS AFTER THEM?"
I'M SURE THAT WOULD WORK OUT PERFECTLY.

STOPPIN' IN WEST VIRGINIA FOR A MOMENT. NEED TO REFUEL. FEEL FREE TO STRETCH YOUR LEGS AND GET SOMETHING TO EAT.
SNACKS!!
YEAH, MIGHT BE A GOOD IDEA.
-duck-
LAST CALL, BUS 48939 LEAVING FOR SEATTLE. PLEASE BOARD NOW.
THAT'S US, COME ON, EVERYONE.
WAIT-- WHERE'S MAGGIE??

STROOMS
MAGGIE!
MAGGIE, STOP!! NO ONE CAN SEE YOUR HAIR!
JUST ONE SECOND. I NEED THAT DINOSAUR!
MAGGIE, NO!
THE BUS IS ABOUT TO LEAVE!
NOOOO, I WANT THE DINOSAUR!
YANK!

NO! NO! NO! I WANT THE STUFFIE!!!
WHICH BUS--
THERE!
VVrrrrrrrrrrrrrr
WAVE
WAVE
...WE'RE TOO LATE.
WE MISSED IT.
MAGGIE, WHAT DID YOU HAVE TO DO THAT FOR?!
WE MISSED THE BUS BECAUSE OF YOU!
AH CRAP.
BUH... BUH...
WAAAHAHAA
I JUST! I JUST! WANTED! SOB! THE STUFFIE! AND--AND--AND--
NGGK!

BUH HUH
I MISS MY **ROOM**!
SOB!
I MISS THE **POOL**! AND I-- I--
THIS ISN'T ABOUT THE **STUFFIE**, IS IT?
-SNRK-
AND WE--CRASHED THE **C-CAR** AND NOW--SOB-- WE MISSED THE **BUS**--AND IT'S ALL MY **F-F-FAULT** AND I JUST I'M SO--SO--SO--
SCARED!
WE CAN'T STICK AROUND. THOSE **F.R.E.A.K.I.S.H.** GUYS MIGHT SHOW UP BEFORE ANOTHER BUS DOES.
WAAHHAAA
BUH HUH.. ..BUH HUH HUH...
WE'RE GONNA HAVE TO **WALK** NOW.
HEY, TINY, IT'S ALL RIGHT.
WE'RE ALL SCARED.
WE'VE BEEN THROUGH A **LOT** THESE PAST FEW DAYS.
snff
IT'S OKAY. WE ALL MAKE MISTAKES, BUT WE'RE GONNA BE ALL RIGHT AS LONG AS WE'RE **TOGETHER**.
WELL... MIGHT AS WELL GET MOVING.
COME ON.
-sniffle-

HOW FAR HAVE WE WALKED NOW?
I DON'T KNOW--THERE'S NO SIGNAL!
I CAN'T EVEN OPEN A MAP. THIS IS--
OH GREAT!
WHAT?
MY O-PAD DIED!
SO NOW NOT ONLY ARE WE LOST, WE WON'T HAVE ANY DIRECTIONS UNTIL WE CAN FIND SOME PLACE TO CHARGE IT!
WHICH COULD BE HUNDREDS OF MILES FROM HERE!
NEWT, KEEP YOUR VOICE DOWN!
KEEP MY VOICE DOWN?? THIS IS THE WORST!!
SHH!
YOU SHH! I DON'T SEE YOU HELPING, OR DO YOU MAGICALLY HAVE A PORTABLE CHARGER HIDDEN IN YOUR FUR?!
QUIET!

LOOK!

WH...WHAT IS THAT??
DO YOU THINK IT'S DANGEROUS?
I DON'T KNOW!
IT'S NOT MOVING... IS IT A **BIRD**?
IT'S TOO **BIG** TO BE A BIRD...
STAY BEHIND ME!
GGGGRRRROOOOAAR!
HAH!
WHAT IS IT??
COME LOOK!

IT'S A **STATUE!!**
SOMEONE PROBABLY PUT IT UP AS A JOKE.
LOOK, IT'S **POINTING!**
MAYBE THAT'S THE WAY TO A TOWN?
I BET IT IS!
THAT THING SCARED THE CRAP OUT OF ME.
PHEW
ME TOO!
ME THREE.
MIGHT AS WELL FOLLOW ITS DIRECTIONS. FIND SOMEPLACE TO CHARGE YOUR O-PAD, NEWT.
YEAH.
LET'S GO!
BUS
3 MILES

WHAT'S THAT LIGHT UP AHEAD?
LOOK! THERE'S THE BUS STATION!!
UGH
OH, THANK GOODNESS--
THERE'S POWER AND WIFI HERE.
tap tap
YAAAAWN

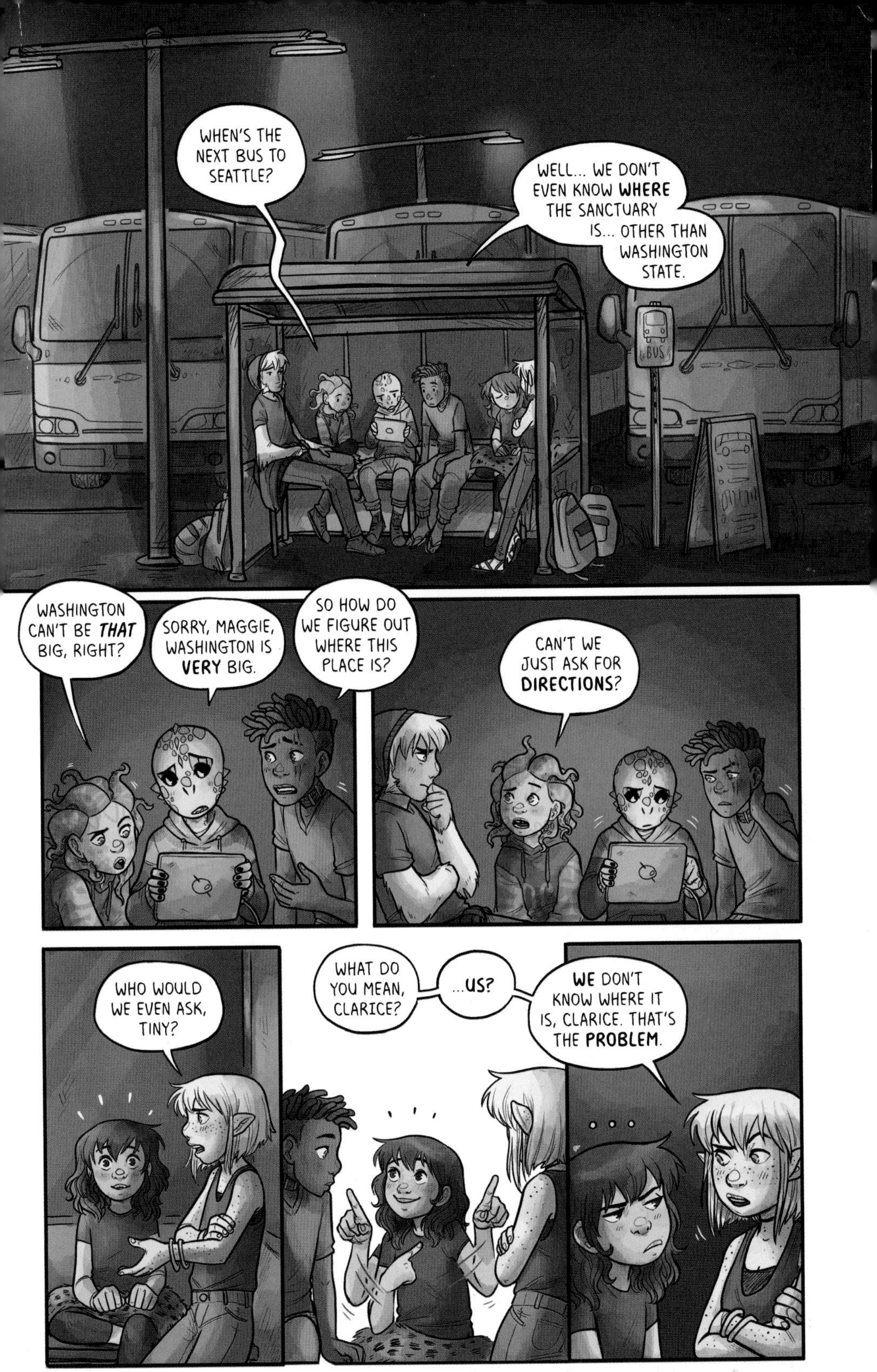
WHEN'S THE NEXT BUS TO SEATTLE?
WELL... WE DON'T EVEN KNOW **WHERE** THE SANCTUARY IS... OTHER THAN WASHINGTON STATE.
BUS
WASHINGTON CAN'T BE ***THAT*** BIG, RIGHT?
SORRY, MAGGIE, WASHINGTON IS **VERY** BIG.
SO HOW DO WE FIGURE OUT WHERE THIS PLACE IS?
CAN'T WE JUST ASK FOR **DIRECTIONS**?
WHO WOULD WE EVEN ASK, TINY?
WHAT DO YOU MEAN, CLARICE?
...**US**?
WE DON'T KNOW WHERE IT IS, CLARICE. THAT'S THE **PROBLEM**.

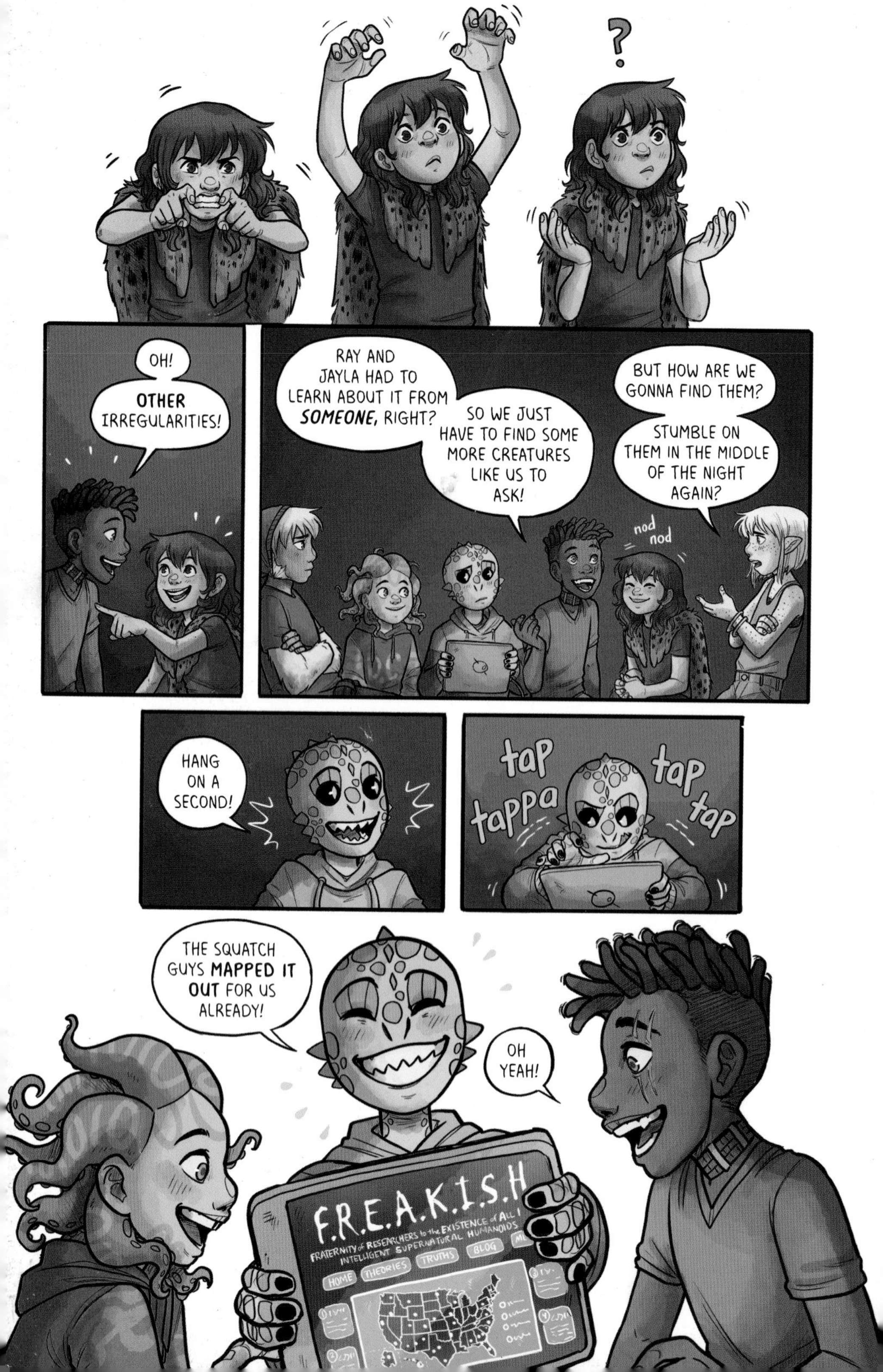
OH!
OTHER IRREGULARITIES!
RAY AND JAYLA HAD TO LEARN ABOUT IT FROM SOMEONE, RIGHT?
SO WE JUST HAVE TO FIND SOME MORE CREATURES LIKE US TO ASK!
BUT HOW ARE WE GONNA FIND THEM?
STUMBLE ON THEM IN THE MIDDLE OF THE NIGHT AGAIN?
nod nod
HANG ON A SECOND!
tap tappa tap tap
THE SQUATCH GUYS MAPPED IT OUT FOR US ALREADY!
OH YEAH!
F.R.E.A.K.I.S.H
FRATERNITY of RESEARCHERS to the EXISTENCE of ALL INTELLIGENT SUPERNATURAL HUMANOIDS
HOME
THEORIES
TRUTHS
BLOG

F.R.E.A.K.I.S.H.
FRATERNITY of RESEARCHERS to the EXISTENCE of ALL KNOWN INTELLIGENT SUPERNATURAL HUMANOIDS
HOME
THEORIES
TRUTHS
BLOG
MERCH
LOVELAND FROGMAN
Loveland, OH
Seems to enjoy scaring tourists. Likely a hoax.
?
THE MOMO
Mississippi River, LA, MO
Short for "Missouri Monster, it has a terrible odor. Super creepy.
?
N
W
E
S
POPE LICK MONSTER
Pope Lick Creek, KY
Half-man half-goat. Very dangerous rumors from various victims!

CHUPACABRA
SW United States and Mexico
Spanish for "Goat Sucker." Known to attack livestock and drink its blood.
?
WA
VISIT AREA51
clack
clack
NEXT EXIT!
F.R.E.A.K.I.S.H.
ALKALI LAKE MONSTER
Walgren Lake, NE
Known to harass swimmers and fishermen. Hasn't been sighted in many years.
?

FRESNO NIGHTCRAWLERS
Fresno, CA
Only seen through pixelated film, these Ghost Pants are thought to be alien life-forms.
LOOK!
WHAT IF THEY REALLY HAVE IRREGULARITIES HERE?
BUS
MUSEUM OF CRYPTIDS
LIVE SPECIMENS
IT WOULD BE A PERFECT COVER STORY, HONESTLY.
CRYPTID MUSEUM
TICKETS
ENTRANCE
LET'S CHECK IT OUT!

WELCOME, TRAVELERS!
COME TO SEE THE TERRIFYING AND BEWILDERING CREATURES FROM ACROSS THE GLOBE?
UH... YEAH.
SIX TICKETS, PLEASE!
TICKETS
ADULT...... $6
CHILD.... $2
SIX TICKETS! COMIN' RIGHT UP!
NICE COSTUME, SWEETHEART! YOU'D FIT RIGHT IN WITH THE EXHIBITS!
SHE NEVER TAKES IT OFF!
HAHA, YEP! HALLOWEEN EVERY DAY WITH HER!
WELL, ENJOY THE SHOW, LIL' LADY!
DON'T GET TOO SCARED, NOW!
ADULT........ $6
CHILD........ $2

THIS IS GONNA BE...
-SNRK-
...TERRIBLE.
?
REPTILIAN
LIZARD-MEN
OCEAN
DEPTHS
SELKIES?
HOAX!
EVIDENCE
FIJI MERMAID
PROOF!
THIS SAYS REPTILIANS EAT **HUMAN FLESH!** GROSS!
SWSH
SWSH

WHY ARE THEY ALL **NAKED**??
Fairies
WHY ARE WHO ALL WHA--
HEY!
YETI
I THINK... I THINK I'M OFFENDED.
SQUEEPLE
YUCK!
LIVE NANDI·BEAR

JAALI?
IS THAT REALLY A NANDI BEAR?
NO, I'M A NANDI BEAR. THAT'S JUST... A BEAR.
A SICK AND OLD BEAR WHO SHOULDN'T BE IN A CAGE!
CLANG
snff snff
whuff
I'M SORRY.
EXIT
GIFT SHOP
THAT WAS... A BAD SHOW.
YEAH.
ARE YOU OKAY?
SNIFF

I THOUGHT... FOR A SECOND...
I THOUGHT IT MIGHT BE **MY DAD.**
YOUR **DAD**??
WHAT HAPPENED TO YOUR DAD?
IT HAD ALWAYS BEEN JUST BABA AND ME. MAMA DIED WHEN I WAS LITTLE. I DON'T REALLY REMEMBER HER.
BABA WORKED FOR THE NATURE PRESERVE--OFFICIALLY AS A RANGER...
BUT WHEN YOU'RE SCARING OFF POACHERS...
...IT DOESN'T HURT TO BE ABLE TO TURN INTO A SEVEN-FOOT BEAR.

BUT THAT DAY...
RAAAAARRGHH!!!
IT'S THEM!
ssshhhfffff
BLAM!
BAM
BAM
BAM
mwwhuuff?!

GGGRRRR
RRRRRR
SWIPE
GGRAAAR!
AGH!
SLASH!
YELP!
huff huff huff
BAM
BAM
huff
huff
HEH, STUPID LITTLE CUB.
hisss

YOU SHOULD HAVE RUN WHEN YOU HAD THE CHANCE.
LET THE COLLECTOR KNOW--WE'VE CAPTURED THE NANDI BEARS.
JAALI... JAALI, WAKE UP.
WAKE UP!!
VVVVVVrrrrrrr
B... BABA...
JAALI, YOU HAVE TO GET OUT OF HERE.
wince
hsss
LOOK, THE SEAM.
IF I WIDEN IT, YOU CAN FIT THROUGH.
BUT WE'LL ONLY GET ONE CHANCE.
BABA, WAIT...
SLAM!
SWERVE
I LOVE YOU. NEVER STOP FIGHTING!

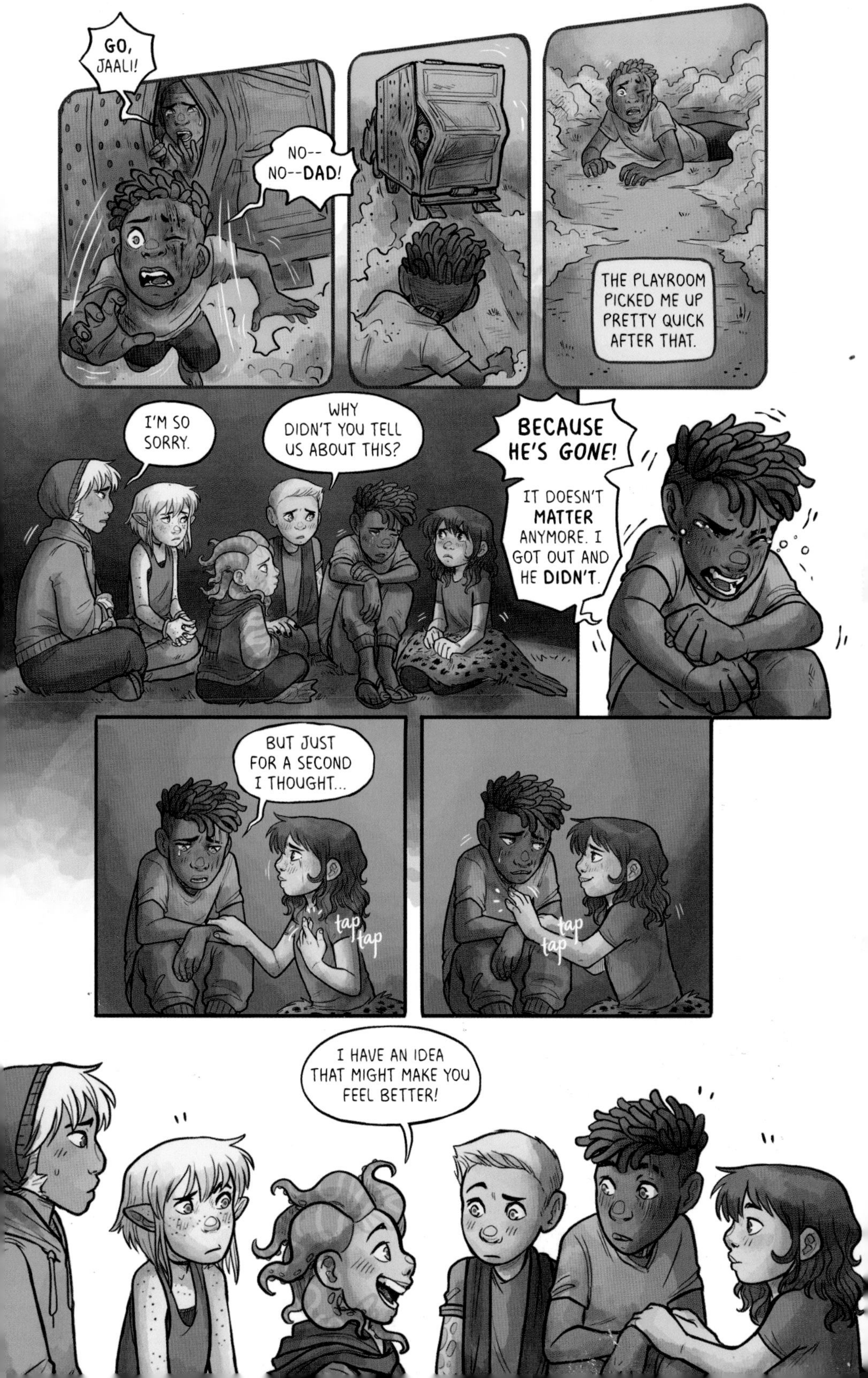
GO, JAALI!
NO-- NO--DAD!
THE PLAYROOM PICKED ME UP PRETTY QUICK AFTER THAT.
I'M SO SORRY.
WHY DIDN'T YOU TELL US ABOUT THIS?
BECAUSE HE'S GONE!
IT DOESN'T MATTER ANYMORE. I GOT OUT AND HE DIDN'T.
BUT JUST FOR A SECOND I THOUGHT...
tap tap
tap tap
I HAVE AN IDEA THAT MIGHT MAKE YOU FEEL BETTER!

GIFT SHOP
chirp
chirp
chirp
chirp
EXIT
CRASH!!

WHAT THE--?!
MY BEAR!!
OR... UM... NOT? MY BEAR? ANYMORE?
GGGRRRRRRRRR

CHAPTER EIGHT

BRIEF RESPITE

WE'VE BEEN WALKING FOREVER--WHY CAN'T WE TAKE ANOTHER BUS??
WE ONLY HAVE ENOUGH MONEY FOR FOOD NOW. CAN'T BUY BUS TICKETS.
RRRUUMBLLLE
OH NO!
FFFFFFSSSSSHHHHHH!!
AHH!
WHAT DO WE DO?!
WE'RE IN THE MIDDLE OF NOWHERE--THERE'S NO PLACE TO GO!

K-K-KRASH!
QUICK--GET UNDER THE TREE COVER!
ISN'T THAT EXACTLY WHERE YOU'RE **NOT** SUPPOSED TO GO DURING A THUNDERSTORM??
JUST GO!!!
K-KRA-KOOM!!
AHH!
RUN!

CRASH!
huff huff
OH MY GOSH!
THAT THING ALMOST HIT US!!
SYLVIE! TURN OUT THE LIGHTS! A CAR IS COMING!
WHAT?!
BRAKE
OH NO!
I DON'T--
SHOULD WE RUN?!
crunch

YOU KIDS ALL RIGHT?!
QUICK--GET IN! THIS STORM IS **DANGEROUS**--NO ONE SHOULD BE OUT IN THIS!
OMAR, WHAT DO WE DO??
C-C-CRASH!!
ANYTHING'S BETTER THAN BEING OUT IN **THIS**!!
JUST GET IN!
FOR
SER

drip
drip
drip
drip
UH... THANKS FOR THE RIDE.
AIN'T NO PROBLEM--WHAT WERE Y'ALL DOIN' OUT HERE ANYWAY??
UHHH... **WALKING**?
HAH, WELL, I GATHERED THAT MUCH! BUT WALKIN' **WHERE**?

...
...
...
AH... I SEE.
NO PLACE TO GO, HUH?
WHY DON'T Y'ALL COME HOME WITH ME? **IRREGULARITIES** SUCH AS YOURSELVES WILL **FIT RIGHT IN.**
I CAN SPOT Y'ALL A MILE AWAY, SEEIN' AS I'M **MARRIED** TO ONE.
HOW DID YOU--??
SINCE YOU GOT NO PLACE ELSE TO GO, MIGHT AS WELL COME TO OUR HOUSE.
I'M SURE MY FAMILY WOULD LOVE TO MEET'CHA.
OR AT LEAST MY WIFE CAN GET Y'ALL SOME DRY CLOTHES AND A HOT MEAL.
WHAD'YA SAY?
SIR...
NO OFFENSE, BUT WE DON'T EVEN KNOW WHO YOU ARE.

INTRODUCTIONS, THEN. I'M RANGER **WILLIAM ANDERSON**, BUT Y'ALL CAN CALL ME **BUCK.**
tip
THAT'S A FUNNY NAME!
SURE IS, HONEY. WHAT'S YOURS?
I'M MAGGIE!
NICE TO MEET'CHA, MAGGIE. Y'ALL GOT NAMES TOO?
I'M OMAR.
JAALI.
NEWT.
I'M SYLVIE.
THIS IS CLARICE.
NICE TO MEET EACH OF YA!
SO WHAT BRINGS YOU TO THE MIDDLE OF NOWHERE IN A THUNDERSTORM?
THAT'S... KIND OF A **LONG STORY**...

...AND THEN YOU FOUND US IN THAT STORM.
Y'ALL BEEN THROUGH THE RINGER.
I AIN'T HEARD OF ANY **SANCTUARY**, BUT MAYBE **ALEX** HAS.
C'MON IN. WE CAN GET YOU SETTLED.
DADDY!
DAD!!
ba ba ba
PICK US UP, DAD!
HA HA HA
HA HA HA
RUNNING LATE TONIGHT, HON?
WELL...
I FOUND A FEW **FRIENDS** AND THOUGHT YOU'D LIKE T'MEET 'EM.
AHH, NIÑOS, YOU LOOK **EXHAUSTED**!
LET ME GET SOME LEFTOVERS HEATED UP.
ISABELLA, MOVE YOUR BLANKETS INTO SAMUEL AND LUCA'S ROOM--WE HAVE **GUESTS**!

MOOOOM, WHY DO I HAVE TO SHARE??
LISTEN TO YOUR MOTHER.
FIIINE.
AY, I CAN'T BELIEVE THIS. YOU'VE BEEN THROUGH SO MUCH.
WELL, IF YOU'RE REALLY HEADING THAT FAR,
MIGHT AS WELL REST UP HERE A FEW DAYS. GET SOME SUPPLIES 'N' SUCH.
IT'S BEEN... A LOT.
YOU'RE NOT GOING TO WALK ALL THE WAY THERE, ARE YOU?
WE'RE HOPING TO TAKE AS MANY BUSES AS POSSIBLE,
BUT THEY GET VERY EXPENSIVE.
IF WE HAVE TO WALK, WE WILL.
YOU ARE SO BRAVE.
ENOUGH TALK FOR TONIGHT--LET'S GET YOU ALL TO BED.
DROOP...
PLAP

WE CAN'T THANK YOU ENOUGH...
HUSH NOW-- SLEEP. WE CAN TALK MORE IN THE MORNING.
PBTTTHHH
HA HA HA HA HA HA HA

EEEEEE!!!
GOTCHA!

JUST EASE HER ON OUT. YOU'VE GOT IT.
HA, CAN YOU TELL I'VE NEVER DONE THIS BEFORE?
YOU'RE DOIN' FINE.
rrrrruumble
BUCK... **THANKS.**
FOR EVERYTHING. FOR LETTING US STAY WITH YOU AND YOUR FAMILY THESE LAST FEW DAYS.
IT'S BEEN SO HARD, TRYING TO TAKE CARE OF EVERYONE WHEN I BARELY KNOW WHAT I'M DOING.
I'MMA LET YOU IN ON A SECRET, OMAR. YOU **NEVER** REALLY FIGURE OUT WHAT YOU'RE DOIN'.
BEIN' AN ADULT IS JUST **WINGIN' IT** UNTIL YOU GET IT RIGHT.
BUT YOU SEEM LIKE YOU HAVE IT ALL FIGURED OUT!
YOUR FAMILY IS **AMAZING,** YOU ALL ARE SO HAPPY, AND YOU'RE--WELL ALEX AND THE KIDS ARE IRREGULARITIES...
LIVING **FREE**.
WELL, AS FREE AS THEY **CAN.** WE STILL CAN'T SEND THE KIDS TO SCHOOL, AND WE GOTTA BE CAREFUL WITH WHO WE TRUST.
FOLKS AROUND HERE CAN BE JUDGMENTAL. BUT HOME IS WHAT YOU MAKE OF IT...
AND FOR US, **THIS IS HOME**.

HEY, ALEX, I HAVE A COUPLE QUESTIONS I'VE BEEN MEANING TO ASK... DO YOU HAVE A MINUTE?
I HAVE SEVERAL! GRAB A BASKET AND GET IN THE DIRT WITH ME.
HAHA, OKAY.
WHAT'S ON YOUR MIND?
YOU AND BUCK AND THE KIDS HAVE BEEN SO WONDERFUL TO US THIS PAST WEEK.
IT'S MEANT A LOT.
BUT WE'RE GOING TO HAVE TO KEEP MOVING SOON, SO I'VE BEEN MEANING TO ASK YOU...
DO YOU KNOW WHERE THE SANCTUARY IS?
SYLVIE... DO YOU REALLY HAVE TO GO? BUCK AND I HAVE BEEN TALKING...
YOU ARE MORE THAN WELCOME TO STAY HERE WITH US. IT'LL BE A TIGHT SQUEEZE FOR A WHILE,
BUT WE'D LOVE TO HAVE YOU ALL AS PART OF OUR **FAMILY.**

AND WE CAN ALWAYS USE MORE HELP AROUND THE HOUSE!
HA HA HA
HA HA
TOSS
THIS COULD REALLY BE A **HOME** FOR YOU ALL.
BUT... IT'S **YOUR** HOME. WE... WE HAVE TO FIND **OUR OWN.**
YOU REALLY THINK THE SANCTUARY IS WHERE YOU BELONG?
WE'VE BEEN SEARCHING FOR IT FOR SO LONG,
AND WE PROMISED TO FIND RAY AND JAYLA.
AND WE WOULD NEVER WANT TO PUT YOUR FAMILY IN **DANGER**.
I UNDERSTAND, SYLVIE, I DO. WE LOVE HAVING YOU HERE, BUT... IF YOU DO DECIDE TO GO, WE HAVE AN OLD FAMILY FRIEND WHO MIGHT BE ABLE TO POINT YOU IN THE RIGHT DIRECTION.
THINK ON IT, ALL RIGHT?

SPLASH
SKIP
SKIP
WHAT'CHA LOOKING AT?
TADPOLES!
THEY'RE BABY FROGS, RIGHT?
plish plish
SORT OF-- THEY'RE A WHOLE **DIFFERENT ORGANISM** WHEN THEY'RE LITTLE!
THESE GUYS HAVE GILLS AND A TAIL, BUT ONE DAY THEY'LL HAVE LUNGS AND **FEET-FINS** AND SAY "**RIBBIT**" AND EVERYTHING!
IT'S AN AMAZING TRANSFORMATION.
THAT'S PRETTY COOL!
YEAH... I DUNNO. I KIND OF IDENTIFY WITH THESE LITTLE GUYS.
LIKE... THEY'RE GOING THROUGH A **BIG CHANGE**. I THINK I'M GOING THROUGH ONE TOO.
WHAT DO YOU MEAN?
SPLISH

I'M PRETTY SURE I'M NONBINARY.
WHAT?
BACK IN D.C.... I TALKED WITH TIBBS. AND THEY HELPED ME REALIZE THAT I CAN IDENTIFY HOWEVER I WANT TO.
AND THE MORE I THINK ABOUT IT... I'M NONBINARY.
trace
OKAY! HOW DO YOU WANT TO BE REFERRED TO?
OH! UH, HE/THEY, PLEASE?
GOT IT. SHOULD WE TELL THE OTHERS?
YOU'RE NOT... MAD?
WHY WOULD I BE MAD??
I DON'T KNOW. IT'S A BIG CHANGE. I JUST THOUGHT--
NEWT.
YOU'RE MY BEST FRIEND.
AND YOU'LL BE MY BEST FRIEND NO MATTER WHAT.
sniff
IF YOU'RE READY, I THINK THE OTHERS WOULD LOVE TO KNOW TOO.
OKAY.

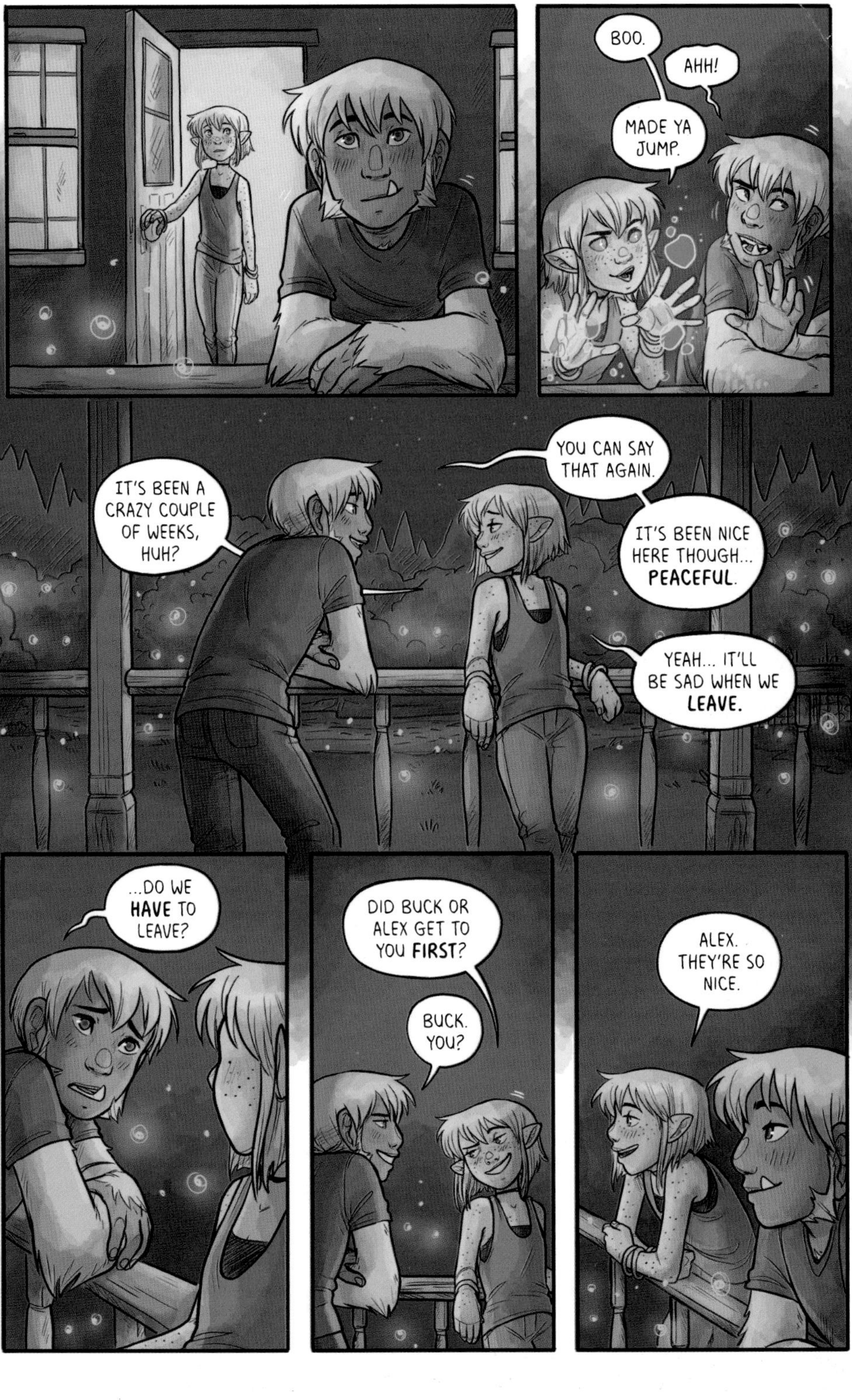
BOO.
AHH!
MADE YA JUMP.
IT'S BEEN A CRAZY COUPLE OF WEEKS, HUH?
YOU CAN SAY THAT AGAIN.
IT'S BEEN NICE HERE THOUGH... **PEACEFUL**.
YEAH... IT'LL BE SAD WHEN WE **LEAVE.**
...DO WE **HAVE** TO LEAVE?
DID BUCK OR ALEX GET TO YOU **FIRST**?
BUCK. YOU?
ALEX. THEY'RE SO NICE.

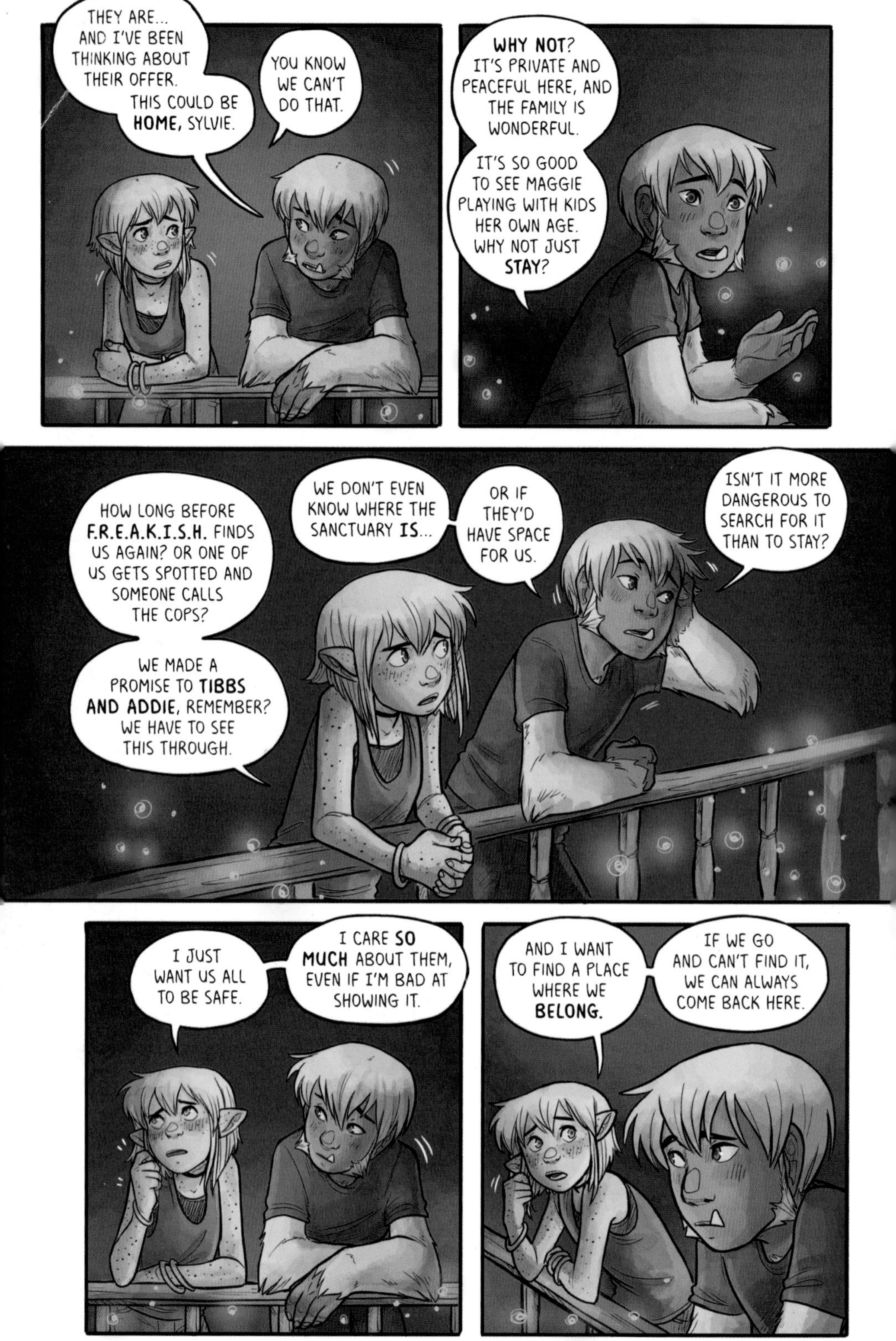

THEY ARE... AND I'VE BEEN THINKING ABOUT THEIR OFFER.
THIS COULD BE **HOME,** SYLVIE.
YOU KNOW WE CAN'T DO THAT.
WHY NOT? IT'S PRIVATE AND PEACEFUL HERE, AND THE FAMILY IS WONDERFUL.
IT'S SO GOOD TO SEE MAGGIE PLAYING WITH KIDS HER OWN AGE. WHY NOT JUST **STAY**?
HOW LONG BEFORE **F.R.E.A.K.I.S.H.** FINDS US AGAIN? OR ONE OF US GETS SPOTTED AND SOMEONE CALLS THE COPS?
WE MADE A PROMISE TO **TIBBS AND ADDIE**, REMEMBER? WE HAVE TO SEE THIS THROUGH.
WE DON'T EVEN KNOW WHERE THE SANCTUARY **IS**...
OR IF THEY'D HAVE SPACE FOR US.
ISN'T IT MORE DANGEROUS TO SEARCH FOR IT THAN TO STAY?
I JUST WANT US ALL TO BE SAFE.
I CARE **SO MUCH** ABOUT THEM, EVEN IF I'M BAD AT SHOWING IT.
AND I WANT TO FIND A PLACE WHERE WE **BELONG.**
IF WE GO AND CAN'T FIND IT, WE CAN ALWAYS COME BACK HERE.

...OKAY. AS LONG AS WE ALL MAKE THE DECISION **TOGETHER**.
HOME... HOME IS WHAT WE MAKE OF IT.
WE SHOULD TALK TO EVERYONE IN THE MORNING.
SYLVIE... I...
I'VE BEEN THINKING...
MAYBE WHEN THIS IS ALL OVER, WE COULD--
SLAM!
WHAT ARE YOU GUYS DOING?
NOTHING!
NEWT'S FINALLY GOT THEIR O-PAD CONNECTED--WE'RE GONNA WATCH A **MOVIE**!
COME IN! LET'S MAKE **POPCORN**!!

KNOCK KNOCK!
WHO THE--
IT'S SO LATE!
BE CAREFUL, CARIÑO.
CAN I HELP YOU?
GREETINGS. WE ARE THE FRATERNITY OF RESEARCHERS TO THE EXISTENCE OF ALL KNOWN INTELLIGENT SUPERNATURAL HUMANOIDS.
WELL, THAT'S A MOUTHFUL.
ALSO KNOWN AS F.R.E.A.K.I.S.H.
WE HAVE REASON TO BELIEVE THERE MAY BE SEVERAL CRYPTIDS NEARBY. HAVE YOU NOTICED ANY STRANGE ACTIVITY?
HOW DID THEY FIND US AGAIN??
GASP!

AIN'T SEEN NOTHIN' AROUND HERE. HAVE A GOOD NIGHT.
WAIT!
IT'S TIME FOR US TO GO.
nod nod
HERE, USE OUR BOAT.
TAKE THE RIVER UNTIL YOU FIND AN OLD FOOTPATH.
FOLLOW THAT AND YOU'LL FIND OUR FRIEND. HE CAN TELL YOU WHERE THE SANCTUARY IS.
BUT BE CAREFUL, MY LOVES!
I'M SORRY WE COULDN'T KEEP YOU LONGER...
IT'S BEEN SO NICE HAVING YOU ALL HERE.
ALEX, **THANK YOU.** THANK YOU SO--
SEARCH THE BACKYARD! HE'S DEFINITELY **HIDING SOMETHING**!
HEY NOW! THIS IS **PRIVATE PROPERTY.** WHO DO YOU THINK YOU ARE?!
THERE'S NO **TIME**, MIS QUERIDOS, **HURRY!**

GET GOING! I CAN MEET YOU DOWNRIVER!
I'LL DISTRACT THEM!
JAALI--!
ANDERSON
RRAAAAGH!
I SHOULDA WARNED Y'ALL. THIS IS **BEAR** COUNTRY!
ROAAAR
THAT'S A **FREAKING** BEAR!
THAT'S A **BEAR**!

ROCK
ROCK
I KNOW IT'S A **BEAR.** WHAT ARE WE GONNA **DO**?!
THERE'S NO MOTOR!
YOU HAVE TO PADDLE-- I'M SORRY!
DON'T APOLOGIZE. YOU'VE DONE SO MUCH FOR US.
STAND
CLARICE?
YOU WANT TO HELP TOW THE BOAT??
nod

YOU'VE GOT THIS.
nod nod
SPLASH
YANK

CLUNK
HNNG!
HUFF HUFF
ARE WE GASP GONNA MAKE IT?
THE RIVER!! SOMEONE'S IN A BOAT!
QUICK!! THEY'RE GETTING AWAY!

PLISH!
HEY, FISHIES!!
WE NEED HELP! COME PUSH THE BOAT!
ANDERSON
sshoooo-Oooom!
sshooooom
THANK YOU, FISHIES! **WHOA**!
THANK YOU, **BIG** FISHIE!

ARE THEY GONNA BE OKAY?
BUCK AND ALEX AND THE KIDS?
THEY'LL BE FINE. THEY KNOW WHAT THEY'RE DOING.
ANDERSON
WHERE'S THE PATH ALEX TALKED ABOUT?
LOOK-- THAT HAS TO BE IT!

SEE ANYTHING YET?
NOT YET.
WHO IS THE "FRIEND" WE'RE LOOKING FOR?
DUNNO, SHE JUST SAID THEY'RE AN OLD FAMILY FRIEND WHO KNOWS WHERE THE SANCTUARY IS.
SHE DIDN'T GIVE YOU ANY MORE DETAILS?
OH, I'M **SORRY,** YOU WANNA GO **BACK** AND ASK HER??
...GRUMPY.
YOUR **FACE** IS GRUMPY!

THIS IS THE WOOOORST!
WORSE THAN WALKING FOURTEEN MILES IN THE DESERT?
OKAY, NOT WORSE THAN THAT, BUT IT'S PRETTY DARN CLOSE. WE'RE **NEVER** GONNA FIND THIS GUY!!
FIND WHO??
rustle rustle
OH MY GOD.
UH... ACTUALLY, SIR,
I THINK WE WERE LOOKING FOR **YOU**.
B-**BIGFOOT**??
YOU LOOK... **FAMILIAR.** HAVE WE MET?
I DON'T BELIEVE SO, BUT IN A WEIRD WAY WE... MIGHT BE **RELATED**?
WELL, I'LL BE DARNED! A **YETI**, HERE IN MY WOODS!
COME ON BACK TO MY PLACE, KIDS.
I'LL GET A KETTLE ON.

SIX IRREGULARITIES, ALL IN MY HOUSE AT ONCE! WHO'DA THUNK, EH?
SO TO WHAT DO I OWE THE PLEASURE?
WELL UH, MR. BIGFOOT, SIR,
ALEX ANDERSON SENT US. SHE SAID YOU MIGHT KNOW ABOUT TH SANCTUARY?
BAH, MORE OF THIS **SANCTUARY** BUSINESS.
EVERYONE COMING THROUGH MY WOODS SEEMS TO WANT TO GET THERE.
YOU KNOW WHERE IT IS?
OH, I KNOW WHERE IT IS, BUT I DON'T TRUST IT FARTHER THAN I COULD THROW IT!
WHY NOT?
IRREGULARITIES GO IN, **NO ONE** EVER COMES OUT!
COULD THAT BE... BECAUSE THEY **LIVE THERE** NOW?
DON'T YOU **SASS** ME, MISSY!
DON'T WORRY, MR. BIGFOOT,
SHE SASSES **EVERYBODY.**

MAYBE IT'S ALL **FAIRY TALES** AND **RAINBOWS**, A BUNCH OF IRREGULARITIES ALL SAFE AND SOUND, TUCKED INTO THAT ESTATE.
BUT I DON'T BELIEVE IT! TOO GOOD TO BE TRUE IF YOU ASK ME.
wiggle wiggle
BUT... WE'VE COME ALL THIS WAY...
PLEASE, SIR, CAN'T YOU JUST TELL US WHERE IT IS?
WE'LL BE CAREFUL.
ALL RIGHT. IT'S AN ESTATE TO THE NORTH. I CAN WRITE DOWN AN ADDRESS.
SOME **RICH OLD MAN** OWNS THE PLACE. NOBODY KNOWS NOTHIN' ABOUT HIM.
YOU'LL KNOW IT WHEN YOU FIND A GATE WITH A **VENUS FLYTRAP** ON IT.
BUT IF EVERYTHING GOES **WRONG**...
...I WON'T SAY I TOLD YOU SO!

CHAPTER NINE

UNRAVELING

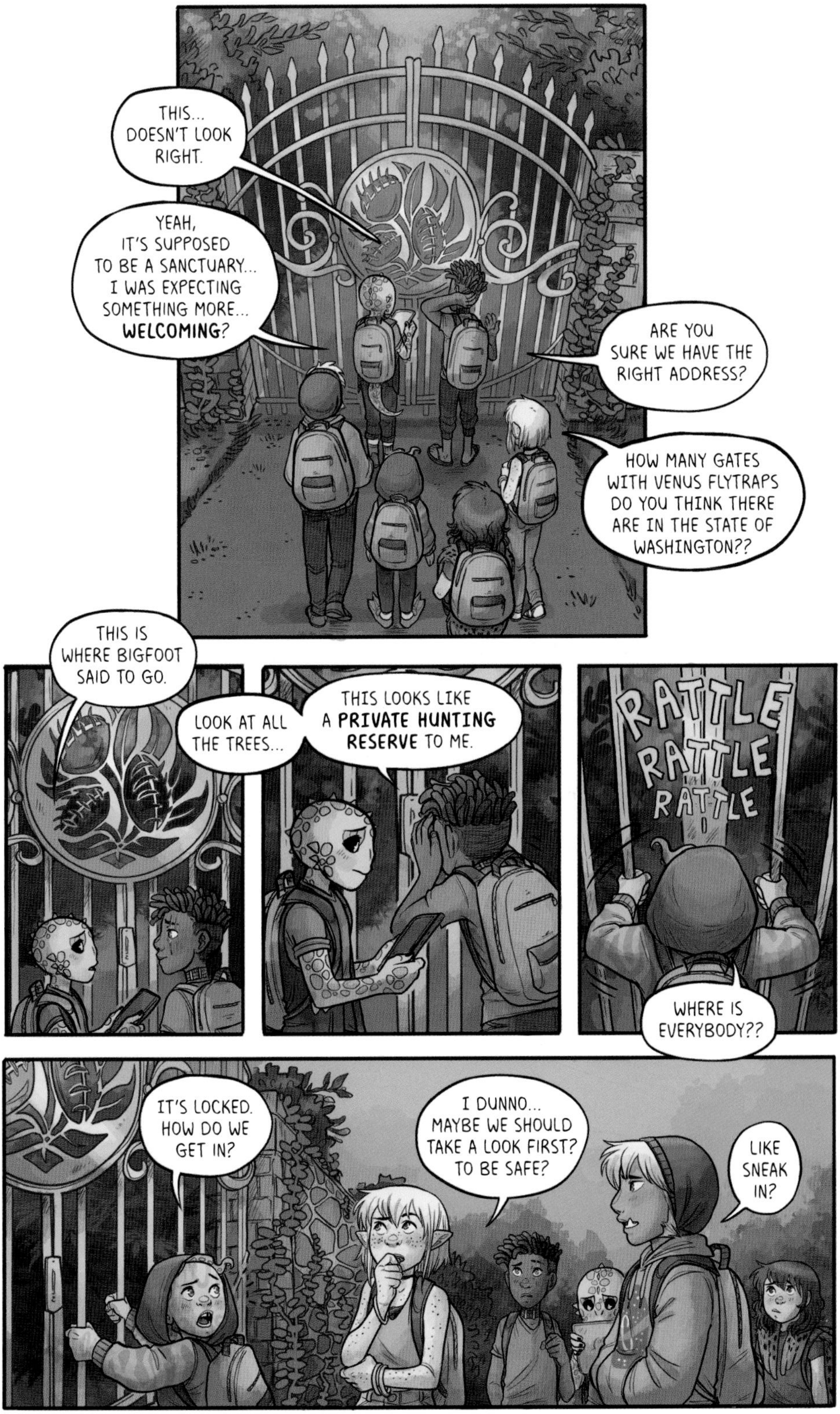
THIS... DOESN'T LOOK RIGHT.
YEAH, IT'S SUPPOSED TO BE A SANCTUARY... I WAS EXPECTING SOMETHING MORE... **WELCOMING**?
ARE YOU SURE WE HAVE THE RIGHT ADDRESS?
HOW MANY GATES WITH VENUS FLYTRAPS DO YOU THINK THERE ARE IN THE STATE OF WASHINGTON??
THIS IS WHERE BIGFOOT SAID TO GO.
LOOK AT ALL THE TREES...
THIS LOOKS LIKE A **PRIVATE HUNTING RESERVE** TO ME.
RATTLE RATTLE RATTLE
WHERE IS EVERYBODY??
IT'S LOCKED. HOW DO WE GET IN?
I DUNNO... MAYBE WE SHOULD TAKE A LOOK FIRST? TO BE SAFE?
LIKE SNEAK IN?

YEAH, SCOUT IT OUT A BIT, Y'KNOW? TAKE A LOOK, IF WE THINK IT'S BAD, WE'LL LEAVE.
I DON'T LIKE THE IDEA OF SPLITTING UP. WHY DON'T WE ALL GO?
OH SURE, MR. SIX FOOT TALL. YOU WANT TO TAKE MAGGIE IN THERE TOO?
I CAN BE SNEAKY!
SHHHHHHHHH!
...I SEE WHAT YOU MEAN.
HERE-- WHY DON'T CLARICE, JAALI, AND I GO CHECK THINGS OUT AND TAKE RAY'S PHONE.
YOU THREE HANG BACK--MAYBE FIND... SUPPLIES OR SOMETHING? IN TOWN?
LIKE SNACKS!!
AND IF ANYTHING GOES WRONG WE CAN SEND A MESSAGE TO NEWT'S O-PAD.
OKAY.
BE CAREFUL, ALL RIGHT???
WE WILL! STOP WORRYING SO MUCH!

GUH! I'M SICK OF WEARING ALL THIS STUFF!
IT'S HOT AND IT SQUISHES MY WINGS!
fumble
QWIK MART 24/7
LOTTERY
HOT!
CHEEZ PLANKS
2 FOR 1
WE'VE TALKED ABOUT THIS--NORMAL PEOPLE WOULD FREAK OUT IF THEY SAW YOU.
I HAVE TO DO MY HUMAN FACE AND HIDE MY TAIL. WE ALL HAVE TO LOOK HUMAN.
BUT THAT ONE GUY THOUGHT I WAS WEARING A COSTUME!
BING BONG
I KNOW BUT HE DIDN'T GET A VERY GOOD LOOK AT YOU. WE JUST DON'T WANT TO GET IN TROUBLE OR SENT BACK TO THE PLAYROOM.
SWIP
SWIP
ONCE WE'RE IN THE SANCTUARY I'M SURE YOU'LL NEVER HAVE TO WEAR IT AGAIN.
...FINE.

I MISS ALEX'S COOKING SO MUCH.
I'M TIRED OF **FROZEN BURRITOS**.
YEAH, ME TOO... LET'S HOPE THIS PLACE HAS SOME **REAL** FOOD.
NEWS
Choco
SKITTIES
SOUR CREAM & ONION
MMM CHIPS!
HOP
HOP
HOP
HNNNNNNG!
ICE
ICE
fwip

MAGGIE!!
SOUR CREAM & ONION
WHAT DID I JUST SAY??
IT'S JUST A BAG OF CHIPS!!
SNATCH
WE CAN'T LET ANYONE SEE YOU! AND THAT INCLUDES YOUR TENTACLES!
WHAT'S WRONG WITH MY TENTACLES?!
NORMAL PEOPLE DON'T HAVE TENTACLE HAIR!
SO... SO I'M NOT NORMAL? IS SOMETHING WRONG WITH ME?

MMM CHIPS!
I'M SORRY, THAT'S NOT WHAT I MEANT.
YOUR HAIR IS **WONDERFUL**. EVERYTHING ABOUT YOU IS WONDERFUL.
IT'S **OTHER PEOPLE** I'M WORRIED ABOUT. PEOPLE ARE... AFRAID OF WHAT THEY DON'T UNDERSTAND.
AND THEY'RE AFRAID OF THOSE WHO LOOK **DIFFERENT.**
MAC
DR. HECK
I DON'T WANNA **HIDE** ANYMORE.
I KNOW. I DON'T EITHER. MAYBE ONE DAY PEOPLE WILL ACCEPT FOLKS LIKE US...
BUT FOR NOW...
SIGH...
OKAY.
YOU READY?
YEAH, LET'S GO PAY.
...GOT TO BE AROUND HERE SOMEWHERE. THE **SIGNAL** KEEPS GETTING STRONGER...
BING BONG
MMM CHIPS

IT'S THEM!
DUCK
QUICK, HIDE!
CLATTER
WHAT THE--?!
IRREGULARITIES!

THAT HAS TO BE THE PLACE.
nod nod
LET'S TAKE A CLOSER LOOK.

I DON'T SEE ANY OTHER PEOPLE... THIS IS **WEIRD.**
I DON'T TRUST THIS. MAYBE BIGFOOT WAS RIGHT?
YEAH, WHAT WOULD A **SANCTUARY** NEED **CAGES** FOR??
MAYBE WE SHOULD GET OUT OF HERE--
...SEEMS EXCITED ABOUT SOMETHING. THOSE **F.R.E.A.K.I.S.H.** GUYS MUST BE GETTING **CLOSE.**

TAKEN THEM LONG ENOUGH. IT'S BEEN **MONTHS**!
INEFFICIENT, IF YOU ASK ME. BOSS SHOULD HAVE SENT **US** OUT INSTEAD.
HE HASN'T SENT US OUT SINCE THAT **KID** GOT AWAY.
SLAM
YOU WOULD THINK AFTER **THREE YEARS** HE WOULD HAVE FORGIVEN US...
HAVE YOU EVER KNOWN HIM TO BE A FORGIVING MAN? LOOK WHAT HAPPENED TO **CLARK.**
GOOD POINT...

C'MON, LET'S GET THE REST OF THESE CAGES LOADED UP.
BOSS WANTS THEM MOVED TO THE SOUTHERN FOREST.
SOUNDS LIKE HE'S GOT PLANS FOR THAT WEREWOLF KID.
RAY!
YEAH, DON'T WANT TO KEEP HIM WAITING.
AGH.
THAT OLD BITE ACTING UP AGAIN?
YEAH, HAVING A CHUNK BITTEN OUT OF YOUR ARM'LL DO THAT.
ALMOST IMPRESSIVE FOR A LITTLE BEAR CUB.
SHAKE
EHH, YOU'VE HAD WORSE. REMEMBER THAT SKUNK APE??
OOF, YEAH, THAT WAS A WILD ONE.
NEVER A DULL MOMENT WHEN YOU'RE WORKIN' FOR THE COLLECTOR!

HOW COULD YOU JUST LET THEM CATCH US, OMAR?!
I DON'T KNOW. I JUST PANICKED! I DIDN'T WANT TO HURT ANYONE!
THEY TOOK OUR BACKPACKS!
IF YOU DO ANYTHING TO MRS. BLUEBERRY YOU'RE GONNA BE IN BIG TROUBLE!!
BANG! BANG BANG!
I CAN'T BELIEVE IT! WE CAUGHT THEM!
...I CAN'T BELIEVE WE CAUGHT THEM.
STUART... I THOUGHT THESE WERE LIKE... CRYPTOZOOLOGICAL ENTITIES, Y'KNOW?
THE MISSING LINK, SCIENTIFIC MARVELS.
BUT I THINK THEY'RE JUST... KIDS.
Homework
Newt's Book

WHAT ARE WE SUPPOSED TO DO, DOYLE? JUST **LET THEM GO**??
WE'VE ALREADY CALLED THEM IN-- THAT COLLECTOR GUY IS **EXPECTING** US!
WE'VE BEEN PAID, WE'VE FOLLOWED THEM ACROSS THE COUNTRY!
WE'RE SUPPOSED TO BE CRYPTOZOOLOGISTS, NOT **KIDNAPPERS**.
KNOCK KNOCK
UHH... WE'RE **KIDS**, YOU'VE **NAPPED US**. BY DEFINITION YOU'RE **DEFINITELY** KIDNAPPERS.
AND YOU TOOK OUR **SNACKS**! WHAT'S THE POINT OF BEING KIDNAPPED IF WE CAN'T HAVE ANY **SNACKS**?!
LET'S PUT IT TO A VOTE. WHO WANTS TO TURN THEM IN?
...
YEAH... I THOUGHT SO.
THEY'RE JUST KIDS, MAN. MONSTER KIDS, BUT KIDS...

SLIDE
HEY... WE WANNA TALK.
snatch
ARE YOU GONNA LET US GO??
LISTEN, SORRY ABOUT ALL THIS... WE'RE JUST TRYING TO DO WHAT WE WERE PAID FOR.
WHO WOULD PAY YOU TO STALK AND KIDNAP A BUNCH OF KIDS?!
CRONCH
WE DIDN'T KNOW YOU WERE KIDS!! WE JUST THOUGHT... I DUNNO. YOU WERE SOME KIND OF INTELLIGENT HUMANOIDS? WHICH, UH, YOU ARE! I MEAN, YOU'RE WAY MORE HUMAN THAN WE THOUGHT YOU'D BE?? OR IS THAT INSULTING? CRAP--
WAY TO GO, BEN.
...SORRY.
WE KNEW YOU'D HAVE TO BE INTELLIGENT, OBVIOUSLY. YOU COULD USE OUR TECHNOLOGY.
WHAT DO YOU MEAN?
WE TRACKED YOU BY TRIANGULATING THE SIGNAL FROM AN O-PAD.

NOT TO SOUND EVEN MORE LIKE A BUNCH OF STALKERS, BUT WEREN'T THERE SUPPOSED TO BE **SIX** OF YOU?
DOES IT **MATTER**?? ARE YOU LETTING US GO OR **NOT**?
WE'RE DEFINITELY LETTING YOU GO. I HAVE A MILLION QUESTIONS TO ASK A REAL LIVE **YETI**, **REPTILIAN**, AND...
OCTOPUS... GIRL?
BUT... YEAH.
WE JUST HAVE TO FIGURE OUT WHAT TO TELL THE COLLECTOR.
THE **COLLECTOR**?!
WELL... YEAH, HE'S THE ONE WHO HIRED US.
WE DON'T KNOW MUCH ABOUT HIM, BUT HIS ESTATE IS A LITTLE NORTH OF HERE.
WE'RE SUPPOSED TO BRING YOU TO HIM. HE'S A COLLECTOR, WE FIGURED HE'S GOT LOTS OF CRYPTIDS.
PLUS HE... --AHEM-- PAID IN **CASH**.
OMAR, OH MY GOD--
IT'S A TRAP.

THAT WAS ME--I'M THE ONE WHO BIT HIM!
THEY'RE THE ONES WHO TOOK MY DAD!
SHH-- WE HAVE TO KEEP QUIET!
THE ESTATE IS WHERE THE COLLECTOR LIVES!
THE SANCTUARY IS A COVER--
HE'S LURING PEOPLE LIKE US HERE, PRETENDING THAT IT'S SAFE--
BUT INSTEAD HE'S COLLECTING THEM--
FOR WHAT?

WE HAVE TO GET IN THERE!
NO, JAALI, WE HAVE TO GET BACK TO THE **OTHERS!**
SYLVIE, MY **DAD** COULD BE IN THERE!
nod nod
ALL THE MORE REASON TO GET **HELP!** WE KNOW NOTHING ABOUT THIS PLACE!
THIS COULD BE OUR ONLY CHANCE TO SNEAK IN UNDETECTED!
OR WE COULD GET OURSELVES ***KILLED!***
tug! tug!
I'LL GO IN **WITHOUT** YOU IF I HAVE TO--
GET **OFF** ME, CLARICE!
AH!
WELL, WELL, WELL.
LOOKS LIKE THE DELIVERY CAME **EARLY!**

GGGGGGRRAAAAAA!
NOT THIS TIME!
DODGE
SWIPE
SLAM!
JAALI!
RUN, CLARICE!
DIVE

LET HIM GO!!
SHE'S A WISP!
DON'T LET HER GET HER HANDS ON YOU!
SNATCH
WHAM
GET THE ONE IN THE BUSHES!
GUUUHHH...
SENT
tremble
GIMME THAT!
HNN!
AAH!
NUH-UH, MISSY. DON'T WANT YOU SLIPPING AWAY!
YANK

LET ME GET THIS STRAIGHT.
YOU'VE BEEN ON THE RUN FOR WEEKS BECAUSE YOU ESCAPED **AREA 51**--
CONTAINMENT 9, ACTUALLY, BUT YEAH, IT'S THE SAME THING.
AND YOU HEARD ABOUT THIS SANCTUARY FOR IRREGULARITIES, BUT IT TURNS OUT IT'S A **TRAP**...
...SET BY THE COLLECTOR--**OUR BOSS**--WHO IS ACTUALLY CAPTURING CREATURES LIKE YOU AGAINST THEIR WILL??
AND NOW OUR FRIENDS ARE IN DANGER. THEY LEFT TO SCOUT OUT THE ESTATE.
BING!
WHAT THE--?
THAT'S MY O-PAD!
OH.. UH, RIGHT, SORRY.
OH NO...
IT MIGHT ALREADY BE **TOO LATE**!
HELKP; TRAP WERR CAGUHT HFELP

WE HAVE TO GO HELP THEM!
I **KNEW** WE NEVER SHOULD HAVE SPLIT UP!
I'M SO ***STUPID!!***
NO, YOU'RE NOT! IF WE WERE THERE WE'D PROBABLY BE CAPTURED TOO.
AT LEAST FROM OUT HERE WE CAN MAKE A **PLAN**!
WE HAVE TO FIND A WAY IN THERE!
BUT **HOW**?! THEY'RE IN TROUBLE. WE HAVE TO DO ***SOMETHING!!***
I THINK WE CAN HELP YOU THERE!
WHAT?? HOW?!
WE'RE SUPPOSED TO DELIVER YOU, RIGHT?
THEY ALREADY KNOW WE'RE COMING...
VVVRRRRRRRRRRRRR
THEY'LL LET US DRIVE RIGHT IN THE FRONT GATE.

CHAPTER TEN

HOME

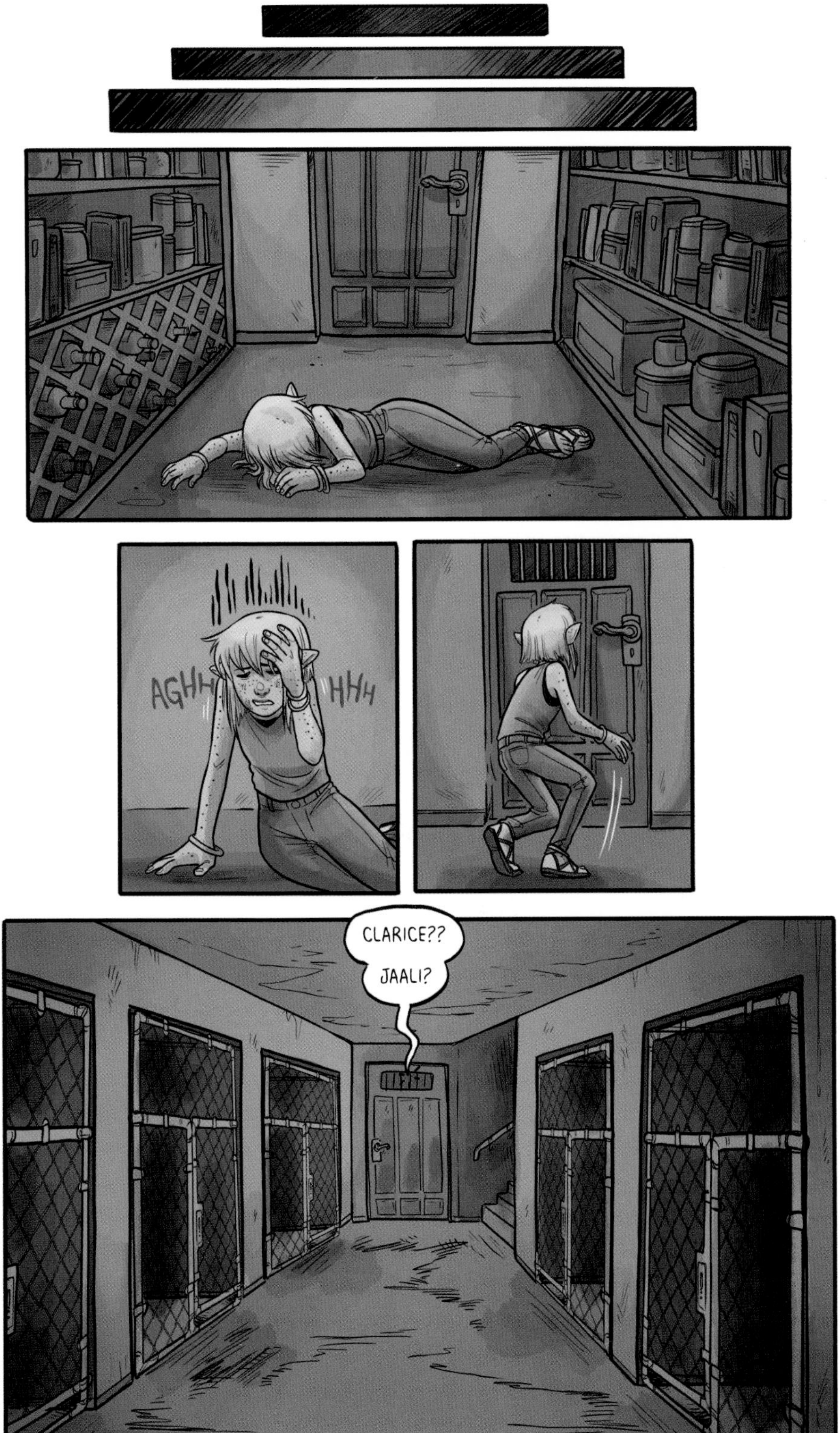
AGHHHHH
CLARICE??
JAALI?

DON'T FRET, LITTLE WISP...
YOU WON'T HAVE TO TROUBLE YOURSELF WITH THEM ANYMORE.
WHO ARE YOU?!
I BELIEVE YOU'VE ALREADY SOLVED THAT PUZZLE, MY DEAR.
YOU'RE THE COLLECTOR?
INDEED. WELCOME TO MY SANCTUARY.
THIS DOESN'T LOOK LIKE A SANCTUARY TO ME. THIS LOOKS LIKE PEOPLE IN CAGES.
WELL... I DID SAY MY SANCTUARY.
IT'S NOT MY FAULT IF YOU THOUGHT IT WAS YOURS TOO.
tp tp
tp
RUSTLE

YOU WANT TO LET ME OUT OF HERE.
YOU WANT TO LET ME AND MY FRIENDS GO!
DROP
LUNGE
THAT'S NOT GOING TO WORK ON ME...
DEAR!
AHH!
SLAM!

WHAT?! HOW DID YOU--?
I'VE BEEN AROUND FOR A VERY LONG TIME, WISP. SUCH WEAK EFFORTS OF PERSUASION WON'T CONVINCE ME.
HA HA HA HA HA HA
HA
WHAT ARE YOU?
HA HA HA
I WAS MUCH LIKE YOU ONCE. A CREATURE TORN BETWEEN WHAT MADE ME HUMAN AND WHAT MADE ME SUPERIOR.
ONE DAY, A HUMAN FOUND ME. DISCOVERED WHAT I WAS.
I'M SURE YOU'RE WELL AWARE OF WHAT HUMANS CAN DO WHEN FACED WITH SOMETHING THEY DON'T UNDERSTAND.
THE IGNORANT BEAST TRIED TO KILL ME, THINKING ME A DEMON OR A MONSTER.
SHE WAS RIGHT.

I LEARNED THAT DAY WHAT I WAS TRULY CAPABLE OF. I COULD **ABSORB THE LIFE FORCE** OF OTHER CREATURES.
WITH THEIR ENERGY, I DIDN'T NEED FOOD OR WATER.
I AGED SO MUCH SLOWER THAN NORMAL HUMANS.
WHEN I UNLEASHED MY TRUE NATURE...
...I WAS **UNSTOPPABLE.**
I GAINED **WEALTH,** I GATHERED **POWER.** I FOUND CREATURES TO COMMAND, TO HELP ME EXPAND MY COLLECTION.
BUT OVER THE YEARS, MY PALETTE GREW TIRED OF THE **MUNDANE**. YOU CAN ONLY ENJOY THE SAME DISH SO MANY TIMES BEFORE IT GROWS TIRESOME.
MY TASTES GREW MORE **GOURMET**.
IRREGULARITIES HAVE SUCH **FLAVOR AND VARIETY,** YOU KNOW.

AND THEY MAKE FOR SUCH **LONG-LASTING** MEALS.
I CAN DRAIN THEM SLOWLY OVER TIME,
WHILE HUMANS MAKE FOR ONLY A QUICK **BITE.**
IS THAT WHAT YOU'RE GOING TO DO TO **US**?
WELL...
NOT **YOU.**
WHAT?
YOU'RE SPECIAL, SYLVIE. **DIFFERENT.** YOU'RE A WILL-O-THE-WISP.
YOU'RE A LOT LIKE ME.
NO!
DOES YOUR INNER SELF NOT CRAVE **CHAOS**?
DON'T YOU WANT TO LEAD OTHERS INTO A TRAP, **BEWITCHING** INNOCENTS TO THEIR **DEATHS**??
IS THAT NOT WHAT WISPS ***ARE?***
IMAGINE YOUR **POTENTIAL**, SHOULD YOU ABANDON YOUR HUMAN WEAKNESS AND ***REVEL IN THE CHAOS!!***
YES!
YESSS!
N-NO...

WE COULD WORK TOGETHER, SYLVIE.
YOU LURE MY PREY TO THIS PLACE, I HUNT THEM.
I'VE ALREADY WRITTEN THE STORY FOR YOU--TELL THOSE WAYWARD CREATURES THAT A SAFE PLACE AWAITS THEM, A SANCTUARY.
THEN LEAD THEM HERE, WHERE THEY WILL FALL RIGHT INTO MY HANDS.
WHAT HAS YOUR HUMANITY EVER DONE FOR YOU?
WHAT HAS HOLDING BACK GIVEN YOU OTHER THAN SUFFERING?
YOU DON'T NEED THESE SHACKLES.
YOU HAVE THE POWER--
SO USE IT!
WELL.
I'VE MADE MY OFFER. REFUSE ME AND I'LL ADD YOU TO THE MENU. THINK ON IT, LITTLE WISP.
BETRAY THE OTHERS. WHO NEEDS THEM?
THEY DON'T NEED YOU...
THIS IS WHAT YOU WERE MADE TO DO...
YOU KNOW YOU WANT TO...
BECOME A FULL WISP,
LET
ME
OUT!
HEE HEE HEE HEE HEE HEE
SMASH!

ARE YOU **SURE** THIS WILL WORK?
OH YEAH, IT'S THE OLD "CAPTURED BY THE GUARDS" PLOY! IT WORKS ALL THE TIME **IN D&D!**
OWWWWW
PUNCH
IT'S THE BEST PLAN WE HAVE. JUST BE READY THE SECOND THE DOOR OPENS.
OKAY!
nod
BEEP BEEP!

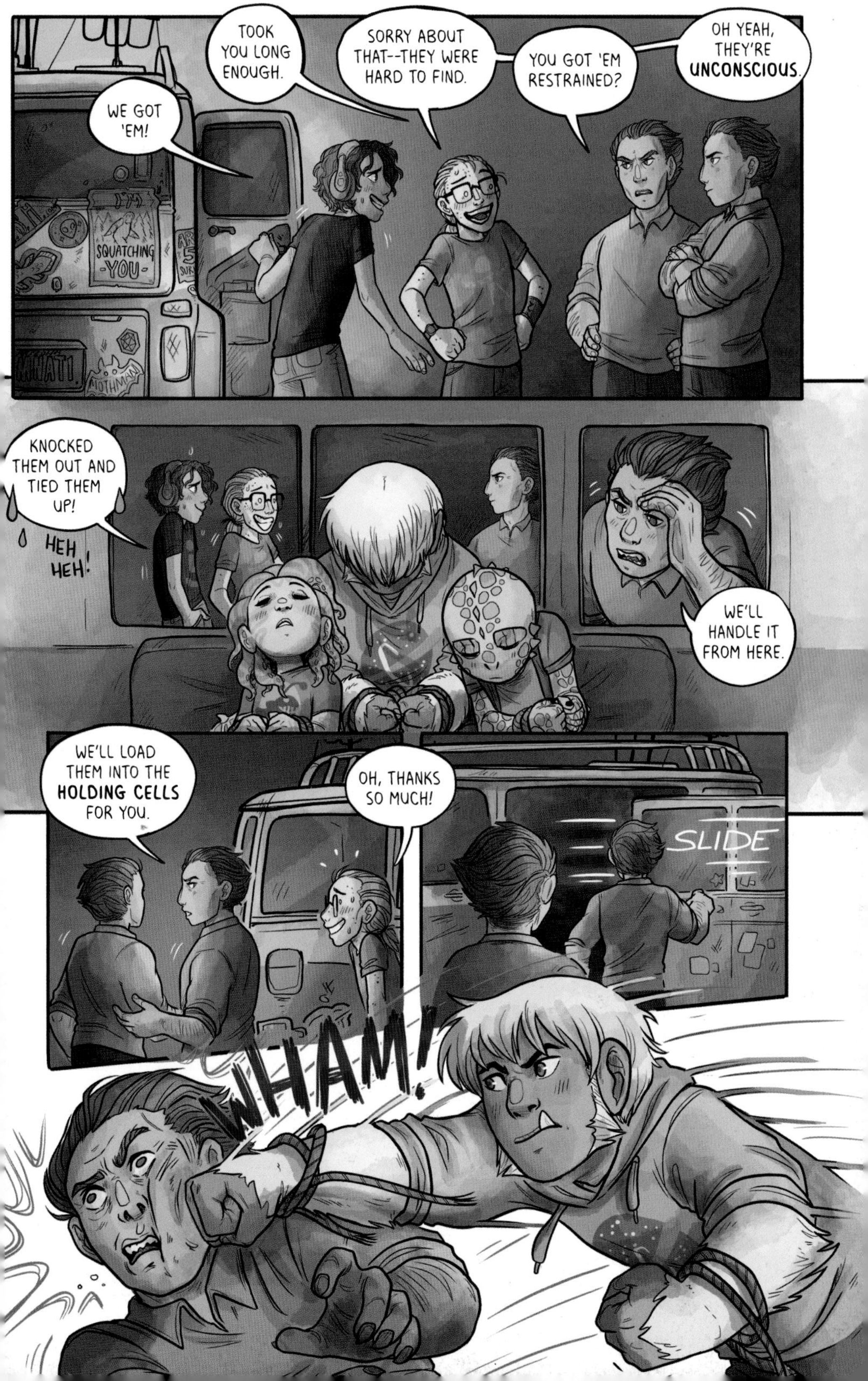

WE GOT 'EM!
TOOK YOU LONG ENOUGH.
SORRY ABOUT THAT--THEY WERE HARD TO FIND.
YOU GOT 'EM RESTRAINED?
OH YEAH, THEY'RE **UNCONSCIOUS**.
SQUATCHING -YOU-
MOTHMAN
KNOCKED THEM OUT AND TIED THEM UP!
HEH HEH!
WE'LL HANDLE IT FROM HERE.
WE'LL LOAD THEM INTO THE **HOLDING CELLS** FOR YOU.
OH, THANKS SO MUCH!
SLIDE
WHAM!

WHUMP!
IT'S AN AMBU--
SCHLORP
GERROFF!
HNNG!
MMPH!
CRACK!

I CAN'T BELIEVE THAT **WORKED**!
FREAKISH
WE DID IT!
QUICK-- LOAD THEM INTO THE VAN SO NO ONE SEES THEM!
NOW WHAT??
WE SNEAK IN!
THEY SAID SOMETHING ABOUT **HOLDING CELLS**. I'M SURE THAT'S WHERE OUR FRIENDS ARE!
CALL RAY'S PHONE! WE CAN LISTEN FOR THE RINGING!
GOOD IDEA, MAGGIE--
COME ON, LET'S GO!

HEY!
LET ME OUT. I HAVE MY ANSWER!
SYLVIE??
WHAT DO YOU WANT?
TAKE ME TO THE COLLECTOR. I'M READY TO JOIN HIM.
WHAT?!
TRAITOR!!
HOW COULD YOU DO THIS?!
AFTER ALL THIS TIME.
WE--WE'RE FAMILY!!

I HAVE TO.
IT'S MY NATURE.
SYLVIE, DON'T **DO** THIS!
RATTLE
RATTLE
SYLVIE, **PLEASE**!!!
SOB
DON'T LEAVE US IN **CAGES**--
GRRAAAAAGH!

CLARICE--
CLARICE, ARE YOU OKAY?
-shudder-
sob
SHAKE
LOOK AT ME--IT'S GONNA BE OKAY.
IT'S JUST **YOU** AND **ME** NOW, AND WE'RE GONNA GET OUT OF THIS.
SYLVIE'S GONE, BUT WE STILL HAVE THE OTHERS--WE JUST HAVE TO GET TO THEM. WE **CAN'T STOP FIGHTING.**
nod
WE'RE GONNA FIND MY DAD AND ESCAPE, OKAY?
STEP ONE--GETTING OUT OF THESE CAGES.

SO...
READY TO JOIN ME, LITTLE WISP?
...YES.
I KNEW YOU'D SEE THINGS MY WAY. WHY DON'T WE GET STARTED?
GOTCHA

DO YOU HEAR IT??
HOW DO WE EVEN KNOW THEY STILL HAVE IT?!
WHUMP
WAIT--
LISTEN!!
SCREEEEEEEEE!
THAT WAY!!
GASP!
INCOMING CALL

NOT WHO YOU EXPECTED, HUH??
HMPH!
tap tap
CRACK!
JAALI!!
HOW DID YOU GET OUT?!
CLARICE PICKED THE LOCKS!
WE'RE SO GLAD YOU'RE ALL RIGHT!

HOW DID YOU GUYS GET IN??
WE HAD SOME HELP FROM OUR NEW FRIENDS.
HI!!!...
EH HEH...
IT'S THE SQUATCH GUYS!!
IT'S OKAY! THEY'RE OUR FRIENDS NOW!
SORRY ABOUT THE WHOLE... STALKING... THING...
...
WAIT, WHERE'S SYLVIE?
SHE'S BETRAYED US.
SHE LEFT TO JOIN THE COLLECTOR.

WHAT?!
SHE SAID IT WAS HER NATURE, AND SHE LEFT.
I GUESS SHE NEVER CARED ABOUT US, IN THE END.
nod nod
THAT...
THAT CAN'T BE RIGHT. SHE'S BAD AT SHOWING IT, BUT SHE CARES SO MUCH ABOUT US--
SHE TOLD ME! TO BETRAY US LIKE THAT-- IT JUST DOESN'T MAKE SENSE.
I DON'T WANT TO BELIEVE IT EITHER...
SHE COULDN'T EVEN **LOOK** AT US WHEN SHE SAID IT.
SHE'S STILL SYLVIE--SHE'S PROBABLY IN TROUBLE!
WE SHOULD HELP HER!
YOU'RE RIGHT--SHE NEEDS OUR HELP.
THIS HOUSE IS MASSIVE. WHERE DO WE EVEN LOOK?!
AND HOW ARE WE GONNA FIGHT THE COLLECTOR?
WE DON'T EVEN KNOW WHAT HE CAN DO!

HE'S A SHADOW BEING--HE CAN SUCK THE LIFE OUT OF YOU.
RAY! JAYLA!
DO WE... KNOW YOU?
HERE--GIMME SOME OF THOSE BOBBY PINS! I'LL HELP UNLOCK THE CAGES.
YOU CAN PICK LOCKS TOO??
OF COURSE I CAN! HOW DO YOU THINK WE KEEP GETTING INTO SECRET FACILITIES?
wink!
WE'RE FRIENDS OF TIBBS AND ADDIE!
THEY'VE BEEN SO WORRIED ABOUT YOU.
AND I THINK...
...THIS BELONGS TO YOU!
I DON'T UNDERSTAND, BUT THANK YOU.

WHAT CAN YOU TELL US ABOUT THE COLLECTOR?
HE'S STRONG, BUT HE CAN'T HANDLE LARGE GROUPS.
THAT'S WHY HE HAS TO GO AFTER HIS PREY ONE BY ONE AND HAS HIS HENCHMEN LOCK US IN THESE CAGES.
DID YOU EVER TRY TO MAKE A BREAK FOR IT?
WE DID, BUT HE'S BEEN DRAINING US FOR WEEKS.
WE BARELY HAVE THE STRENGTH TO USE OUR POWERS NOW.
SOME PEOPLE LAST FOR MONTHS, EVEN YEARS, BUT MOST WASTE AWAY INTO HUSKS AFTER HE DRAINS THEM.
I THINK IF WE ALL WORK TOGETHER, WE MIGHT BE ABLE TO BEAT HIM.
HEY, GUYS? SOME OF THESE PEOPLE ARE REALLY WEAK...
DAD!!!

JAALI!!
I THOUGHT I'D NEVER SEE YOU AGAIN.
BABA...
I'VE MISSED YOU SO MUCH!
HOW ARE YOU EVEN HERE? I--OH, SON, I'M SO PROUD OF YOU.
I HAVE SO MUCH TO TELL YOU.
WE STILL HAVE TO FIND SYLVIE!
I CAN TAKE YOU TO THEM.

YOU MONSTER--
YOU **REALLY** THOUGHT I WOULD JOIN **YOU**?!
TREACHEROUS LITTLE **IMP**, I'LL END YOU HERE AND NOW!
YOU **HIDE** BEHIND YOUR POWER, FATTENING YOURSELF UP WITH OTHER PEOPLE'S LIVES!
I AM **UNSTOPPABLE.** I HAVE LIVED LONGER THAN ANY BEING IN THIS WORLD!
BUT YOU LIVE BY **KILLING OTHERS**!
LOOK AT ALL THE **LIVES** YOU HAVE **DESTROYED**!
STOP IT! THIS ISN'T **REAL**-- I KNOW YOUR TRICKS, WISP!

LOOK AT THE **FAMILIES** YOU'VE RIPPED APART--
LIKE YOU'RE TRYING TO RIP APART **MINE!**
THIS ISN'T REAL--THEY ARE MINE! I REGRET **NOTHING!**
YOU REGRET **EVERYTHING.**
YOU'RE A **COWARD.**
WILLING TO SACRIFICE **ANYTHING** TO PROLONG YOUR OWN LIFE.
YOU ARE TRULY **ALONE!!**
YOUR TIME IS **OVER,** COLLECTOR!
ENOUGH!

LITTLE FOOL, WHO DO YOU THINK YOU ARE?!
I HAVE LIVED COUNTLESS LIFETIMES, CONSUMED THOUSANDS, AND YOU THINK SOME PRETTY ILLUSIONS WILL BEST ME?!
YOU ARE PATHETIC,
PROTECTING OTHERS BY SACRIFICING YOURSELF--
DENYING WHAT YOU ARE TO THE VERY END!
YOU COULD HAVE BEEN LIKE ME. POWERFUL, STRONG, IMMORTAL!
SHHNNGK
I... AM... NOTHING... LIKE YOU!
hissssssssss

SYLVIE!!
HOW DID YOU--?!
NO!
GASP!
GUARDS!

GRAB YOUR FRIEND--
WE'LL TAKE THE GUARDS!
fwip!
fwip!
SLAM
fwip

GRAH!
DODGE
SEIZE HIM!
YANK!
CLING

YOU FOOLS! I WILL DRAIN YOU ALL!
AGH!
shoom
RRRAAAGH
YOU'LL NEVER HURT ANYONE EVER AGAIN!!
HOLD HIM DOWN!
NO!
OMAR!
I'M OKAY-- GO GET SYLVIE!

I TRIED...
SYLVIE--
I TRIED...
IT'S NO USE...
SYLVIE, GET UP!
...HE'S TOO STRONG...
GET UP, SYLVIE!
WE NEED YOU!
...HELP ME UP.
RELEASE ME!
I WILL NOT BE DEFEATED BY MERE CHILDREN!
I AM IMMORTAL!
I AM UNSTOPPABLE!
THIS IS WHAT YOU'LL NEVER UNDERSTAND, OLD MAN.
FAMILY PROTECTS ONE ANOTHER...

...AND LOVE IS STRONGER THAN ANY SHADOW.
NO!
NO!
NO!
NOOOOOOO!!!

SYLVIE!
SLUMP
ARE YOU OKAY??
I'M ALL RIGHT, JUST EXHAUSTED.
HOW DID YOU **DO** THAT??
I COULDN'T HAVE DONE IT WITHOUT YOU ALL...
THANK YOU FOR RESCUING ME. I'M SORRY I HAD TO TRICK YOU.
YOUR BEST TRICK YET.
FAMILY PROTECTS ONE ANOTHER RIGHT?

I FOUND YOUR BANGLES, SYLVIE.
I DON'T THINK I'LL BE NEEDING THOSE ANYMORE. WHY DON'T YOU WEAR 'EM FOR ME?
WOW, REALLY??
YOU **SAVED** US. I KNEW YOU WOULD.
I THOUGHT I WAS GOING TO LOSE CONTROL...
YOU? **NEVER.**
SHUT UP, YOU DUMMY.

Y'KNOW... THIS PLACE IS REALLY BEAUTIFUL WHEN IT'S NOT A **SHADOW MONSTER'S HUNTING GROUNDS**.
WHAT ARE WE GONNA DO NOW?
THE COLLECTOR'S GONE... WHAT IF WE MADE A ***REAL*** SANCTUARY?
MAYBE **THIS** COULD BE OUR HOME.
I LIKE THE SOUND OF THAT.
I DON'T CARE **WHERE** HOME IS...

...AS LONG AS WE'RE TOGETHER.

THE VERY FIRST DRAWINGS OF THE MAIN CHARACTERS.

THIS IS RETCH! ONE OF THE ORIGINAL CONCEPT CHARACTERS, BUT HE DIDN'T MAKE IT TO THE FINAL VERSION.

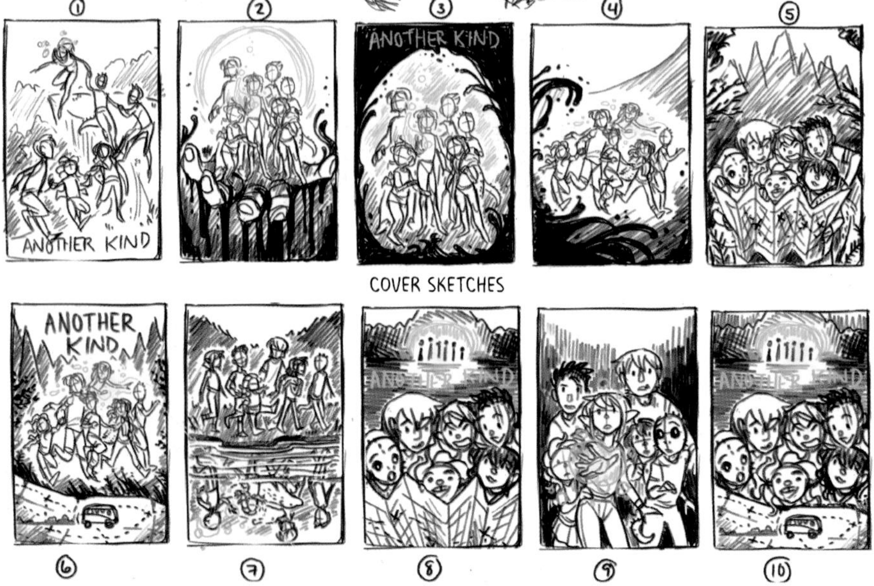

COVER SKETCHES

ACKNOWLEDGMENTS

THANK YOU TO OUR FRIENDS AND FAMILY FOR THEIR UNENDING SUPPORT AND ENTHUSIASM THROUGHOUT THE CREATION OF THIS BOOK. YOU KEPT US GOING AND INSPIRED SO MANY OF THE FAMILIES IN THIS STORY. WE LOVE YOU!

THANK YOU A MILLION TIMES OVER TO SAVANNA AND GIGI—OUR UNBELIEVABLY AMAZING FLATTERS WHO MADE THIS BOOK POSSIBLE THROUGH THEIR PATIENCE, PERSERVERENCE, AND DEDICATION TO THE MEME. BDB FOREVER.

THANK YOU TO CLAIRE, THE AGENT OF OUR DREAMS, WHO GEEKED WITH US THE WHOLE TIME AND IS MAGGIE'S #1 FAN IN THE ENTIRE UNIVERSE. THANK YOU FOR HELPING US MAKE THIS HAPPEN.

THANK YOU TO ROSE, ANDREW, AND JOE AT HARPER FOR BEING THE BEST TEAM WE COULD ASK FOR! Y'ALL ARE CHAMPIONS AND WE CAN'T WAIT FOR THE NEXT.

THANK YOU TO OUR HOME OFFICE FURRY COWORKERS FOR ALWAYS LAYING ON US WHEN WE WERE TRYING TO GET WORK DONE. MANY SCRITCHES AND PETS FOR YOU.

SHOUT-OUTS TO THE DIPPERS—OUR FIRST AND BIGGEST FANS. THANK YOU JOAN HILTY, ALEX FINE, THE ELDRITCH CREW, THE GIRL* GANG, THE PEPPER PAUPERS, LOREN COLEMAN, AND THE CRYPTOZOOLOGY MUSEUM. THANK YOU TO *BUZZFEED UNSOLVED*, *THE ADVENTURE ZONE*, *CRITICAL ROLE*, AND WAY TOO MANY PODCASTS FOR HELPING KEEP OUR MINDS OCCUPIED THROUGH THE TOUGH TIMES.

TO ALL THE CRYPTOZOOLOGISTS WHO HAVE COME BEFORE US. WITHOUT YOUR DEDICATION TO THE STUDY OF WEIRD PHENOMENA, WE MIGHT NEVER HAVE LEARNED TO LOVE THEM JUST LIKE YOU DO.

AND FINALLY—
THANK YOU FOR READING!

FOR DOYLE
AND FOR OUR FAMILIES,
OF ONE KIND OR
ANOTHER

HARPERALLEY IS AN IMPRINT OF HARPERCOLLINS PUBLISHERS.

ANOTHER KIND
COPYRIGHT © 2021 BY CAIT MAY AND TREVOR BREAM
ALL RIGHTS RESERVED. PRINTED IN CANADA.
NO PART OF THIS BOOK MAY BE USED OR REPRODUCED IN ANY MANNER WHATSOEVER WITHOUT WRITTEN PERMISSION EXCEPT IN THE CASE OF BRIEF QUOTATIONS EMBODIED IN CRITICAL ARTICLES AND REVIEWS. FOR INFORMATION ADDRESS HARPERCOLLINS CHILDREN'S BOOKS, A DIVISION OF HARPERCOLLINS PUBLISHERS, 195 BROADWAY, NEW YORK, NY 10007.
WWW.HARPERALLEY.COM

LIBRARY OF CONGRESS CONTROL NUMBER: 2021939648
ISBN 978-0-06-304353-4 (PBK.) — ISBN 978-0-06-304354-1

TYPOGRAPHY BY JOE MERKEL

22 23 24 25 TC 10 9 8 7 6 5 4 3 2

❖

FIRST EDITION